Pike's Quest

K J Bennett

Cover design - K J Bennett

This is a work of fiction. In fact, it's total fantasy. Any resemblance to persons living or dead is not only coincidental, but also highly unlikely. No horses or rabbits were harmed during the writing of this novel.

Don't forget to moisturise!

www.kjbennett.co.uk

ISBN: 1467927694
ISBN-13: 978-1467927697

*

Dedication

To my wife Theresa:

All my love, and thanks for putting up with me.

Acknowledgments

I would like to thank my brother, **Paul Hennessey**: without his original idea, Pike may not exist.

Also, many thanks to the members of **Verulam Writers' Circle** who sat, listened and laughed as I read sections out loud to them. Find them at www.vwc.org.uk.

Mostly, thanks to all those wonderful souls who have already read the Kindle edition of ***Pike's Quest*** (especially those who paid for it!) and to the readers who took the time to review it on the Amazon websites, Goodreads.com and other assorted outlets. It is for people like you that I write my (silly) stories.

Pike's Quest - Contents

1: THE FERTILITY STONE OF OOZE

The Longest Day – Summer 902 ND

Grey and jagged, and tinged with the orange glow of the low morning sun, it stood no more than three adult feet high. It was hardly impressive, but the villagers believed it had been the source of many a pregnancy in the tiny hamlet of Ooze.

It was just after dawn when the small figure cautiously trod the path, which was no more than soil compressed by the feet of thousands. He could see its pointed top above the low-lying mist of a humid summer morn, and he wondered why he had been sent there. His feet sliced through the vapour: he looked back over his shoulder, seeing that it curled in behind him, blocking his view of the trail.

The boy reached his destination and stood next to the stone in anticipation.

Forty smaller slabs, flat and round, formed a perfect circle, with the fertility stone at its centre. The radius was thirty adult feet. As the mist swirled, he could just make out the shape of the circle, but not the individual stones. It was as if they sent out invisible blades to cut their boundary through the blur. A dense forest surrounded the clearing.

Apprehensively, the boy draped a dirty sack over the stone and gingerly placed his backside upon it.

Two hours passed, and things were getting uncomfortable. He stood, doubled the sack, and draped it over the stone once more. Another hour passed: he folded the sack over again to create an even thicker barrier against the sharp edges. When the sun was at its highest, and sweat beaded on the boy's forehead, dripping into his eyes over his not-yet-bushy-enough eyebrows, a dark figure emerged from the woods, shuffling towards him along the well-trodden path.

It was an elderly man with a long, dark-grey beard and a pronounced stoop. A floppy, pointed hat sat on his head. Roughly cut hair in straggles and clumps jutted out from under it. His face was grizzled and weather-beaten and caked with grime. He supported himself with a gnarled and knotted length of wood, which had the appearance of having been hewn directly from a tree, bark and all. It was the height of a fully grown man, standing a good child's foot taller than its stooped keeper. He looked inquisitively at the boy on the stone and stopped close by.

"You're sitting on the fertility stone," he said.

"I know."

"Why?"

"Mother said I'd need all the help I could get for later life. I don't know what she meant. It's a good job I brought this sack." He wriggled his bum to ease the pressure.

The old man's jaw dropped, displaying unusually white teeth, like the polished whalebone ornaments sold by passing traders. The sight of them belied his otherwise vagrant-like appearance.

"How old are you, boy?"

"I am in my seventh year. Today is my birthday. It hasn't been much fun, so far."

The scruffy old man looked shocked. "Can you really be the one? Your seventh year, eh? And are you the seventh son of a seventh son?"

"I think I am," replied the boy. "I've got lots of brothers and many uncles. I don't know what you're getting at, though."

"Oh."

"Why 'oh'? And why are your teeth so white?"

"I am Quentin Moorlock, the County Warlock – and that should answer your question about my teeth. I said 'oh' because there is a problem, an insurmountable one."

"What's the problem? And what does insum ... insir ... insmontacle mean?"

Moorlock the Warlock pushed down on his staff and un-stooped himself, standing at even height with it. "It's a problem, my lad, because it's noon on the longest day, and you are sitting on that stone. That gives you a role that in later life you must fulfil. It's insurmountable – yes, that's the correct way to say it: in-sur-mount-able – because normally in these situations we expect our champions to be of higher pedigree and, dare I say, a little less fishy."

The boy glared at the old man, his mouth opening and closing. A sharp lump blocked his throat, stopping his words from forming. He scratched his head, causing flakes of dry skin to fall onto his sackcloth clothing, and managed to say, "You think I'm fishy?"

"Let's put it this way: if ever modern scholars needed proof positive that all life originated from the ocean, then that proof sits before me. On a stone. The fertility stone. At noon. On midsummer's day. Look at the way your mouth opens and closes, like a fish: and that skin condition – fish scales, it looks to be. So, what's your name, my pseudo-aquatic friend?"

"Pike", he sobbed. "But you're not my friend and I don't know what sue dough means,"

"Ha! This gets better and better. Pike: fish by name, fish by nature. This can't possibly work."

"Whatever it is, I don't want to do it, anyway," said Pike, his tears forming. "And I'm not fishy."

"Yes you are. But, fish or no fish, you must follow your destiny. Meet me back here in the year of your sixteenth birthday, same time, same stone. And don't forget to moisturise."

He turned to leave, but then paused and looked back over his shoulder. "Don't take it to heart, young man, I'm sure that when you get home, your mother will console you. Pike, she'll say, of course you don't look fishy."

Pike huffed, sliding off the stone and grabbing his old sack. "She don't call me Pike; she calls me Tiddler, 'cos I'm little."

With a hoot of laughter, Moorlock the Warlock walked away.

Early Summer – 911 ND (Nine years later)

Spring eased into summer: blooms bloomed, the flies flew, and birds stole seed and shoots from the recently sowed fields. The hamlet of Ooze was alive with the bustle of the market – and a horse.

The horse rampaged up and down the track that divided the hamlet of Ooze in half. People screamed and scattered as it succeeded in demolishing the fruit and vegetable stall by rearing up and belly-flopping onto it. It moved on to the butcher's wagon, from which a host of blue-bottles beat a hasty retreat when the wild stallion again raised up on its hind legs, bringing its fore-hooves down onto the rancid display of blood and offal. By demolishing these two displays it destroyed the market in its entirety. The horse walked calmly away and began to nibble thatch from the roof of a small wattle and daub building. Crushed vegetables dripped from around its belly whilst it chomped.

A worm-holed shutter burst open, smashing against the wall, splintering at its hinges and causing the horse to bat a single eyelid before pulling off a large strip of thatch and wolfing it down in one.

"Get off thur! Ya rabid ol' mule," screeched the old crone from out of the window, drowning out the cries of distress from the two stallholders and their nine customers.

Seething with rage, the crone, ravaged by age and a hard life, inadvertently spat a tooth at the horse, to no good effect.

"Argh! T'were me last tooth, t'were. Gi'it back, ya filthy 'oss!" she screeched.

Nonchalantly, the horse turned away and wandered off along the deeply scarred track, apparently satisfied with its morning's work.

"PIKE? PIKE? Ya need to mend me roof! That blessed mule's eaten it again." She spat blood out of the window and slammed shut the shutter. The final splinters holding it in place gave way. It fell into a dried-up rut, smashing as it landed.

"Now 'ee's broken me shutter, an' all!"

Pike stepped into the small house from the doorway in the back wall. He'd heard the commotion but hadn't bothered to venture around the front to investigate. Why should he? It happened so often it was obvious what was going on. He glanced over at the old woman.

"I told you not to slam that thing, didn't I?" He scratched his chin; flakes of dried skin cascaded onto the straw-covered floor. "And I said not to speak of that creature like that. You'll have the wrath of the gods bearing down on you."

"Ya told us no such tripe, yoom idiot, boy! Ow's I gonna sleep wi'that thing open all night, eh?"

"It's all right, Grandma," he sighed. "I'll fix it on again."

"And the roof?"

"Yep, and the roof."

"Ah, thur's moy little Tiddler! Ee's notsa big as he forgets his ol' Gran, is ee?" She stepped towards him, arms outstretched for a hug, shrivelled lips puckering for a kiss, blood and spittle oozing from their corners.

Pike dodged around her, taking three short paces from the centre of the room to the open window. "Oh, Grandma! Don't be soft! And why do you talk like that, anyway? No one else round here talks like you do."

"Lived 'ere all me loife, I 'ave: babe, an' girl an' woman an' all. How many others round 'ere can say that, eh?"

"Hmm, difficult … let me think … yep! Got it: every fully-grown woman in Ooze. No one moves in, no one moves out. We've all lived here, all of our lives."

"Bah!" snapped the old woman. "Always the same argument. I'm goin' t'moy room."

"You're in your room. This is it, there's nothing more. Ground floor yours, upstairs for visitors. Not that you get any."

"Well I'll take t'moy bed, then," she huffed, sitting on a low, sack-covered pile of straw that lay behind a rough, wooden ladder, which led up to a rickety platform in the roof-space.

"You do that, Gran. I'll nip home and get my tools."

Pike left by the rear door and headed to his home, about forty adult feet away.

He reflected on his Grandmother's words. Tiddler, she'd called him. Hadn't heard that in a while. He was always called Tiddler, when he was smaller, and he thought it to be a term of endearment. That is, until the day he met Moorlock the Warlock at the fertility stone. Since then he'd wondered about it; he wondered even more when he reached his fourteenth year and everyone except for Grandma started to call him Fish.

Pike arrived home. From behind a water butt at the back of the small homestead he grabbed a calfskin bag containing his tools and then went around the front of the house to find his mother. She was sitting on an upturned bucket, chewing on a piece of straw and gazing idly into space. Remembering Moorlock's words he could contain himself no longer.

"I heard that all life started in the ocean."

His mother, a thickset woman with lank, dark hair, wearing a long sack-cloth dress, a white apron and half a watermelon skin as a bonnet, looked at him and sighed. "Oh? So how did we get here, eh? The ocean is many miles from here: fish don't have legs, and whoever heard of a flying fish? It's nonsense, boy. Don't know where you get these ideas."

"What about me: am I fish-like?"

His mother spluttered. "Get away with you lad: fish-like? You? Nah! Well, erm … actually, and I know that as a loving mother I shouldn't really say this … but … erm … errrr …. ackkhhhh! No, o'course not."

"So why does everyone call me Fish?"

"Because you were my little tiddler, and now you're all growed up!"

"But a tiddler is a small–"

"Fish! I know, I know, but it wasn't meant like that. Why, you were just a small babe, you were. You were my little tiddler … so helpless and tiny." A nostalgic tear rolled down her left cheek.

Pike's mouth opened and closed, but words failed to come out. He was often struck dumb by parental logic.

His mother glared at him. "Stop gaping, boy. You look like a trout!"

Spurred on by the insult, the question that had haunted him for more than half of his life bubbled to the surface.

"Er, Mum, what's an ocean?"

The Longest Day – Summer 911 ND

The days grew longer and the weather became warmer. In the time leading up to Pike's birthday he often found himself sitting by the wide pool that was fed by the River Ooze, trying to catch his reflection in the water, wondering if one day he would sprout gills and swim away with other fishy folk. After trying this three times without success, he decided to try it again, but this time in daylight, just to see if that made a difference.

A little after dawn on the longest day of the year, his birthday, Pike cast the best reflection of himself he had ever seen. The low sun was strong enough to highlight even the tiniest detail of his face.

He stared into the water in disbelief, his mouth opening and closing several times before his words formed. He didn't know what the worst part was: the bulging black eyes, the trout-like mouth, or the chronic dry skin condition that caused his epidermis to crack up like fish scales.

"By the power of Adriarch the Sinner: I'm as ugly as a carp that's had its brains splattered on a rock!"

He rubbed his chin in wonderment. Flakes of skin sprinkled onto the water, slightly obscuring the image. A small fish bobbed to the surface to devour them. Before it could sate its hunger it caught sight of Pike and darted off in horror. From the distant reaches of Pike's memory, some words echoed:

Don't forget to moisturise.

The words of Moorlock the Warlock.

It was only then that he remembered that today was the day he must revisit the fertility stone.

Just before noon, Pike plonked his backside on the stone. It seemed much smaller than it had all those years before. Mind you, he was much tinier the last time he'd sat there, so he hadn't realised just how sharp and pointy it was. Still, keeping to his word, he sat on the stone and awaited the arrival of the Warlock, wishing that this time he had brought more than one sack to cushion his rear.

It was an hour later when a bird landed on his shoulder.

"Be gone, blasted sparrow!" shouted Pike.

"Shut up, fish-face," snapped the sparrow, much to Pike's surprise. "Holy Herne the Hunter! Moorlock was right. This is totally insurmountable. No way are you suited to the quest. Deal's off. Bye-ee!"

The sparrow raised its wings as if to leave.

"Quest? What quest?"

"The quest to release Moorlock from eternal damnation at the clutches of his arch enemy, and then to win the heart of the fair maiden in the Pit of Zidor, that's what quest, stupid."

"That sounds like two quests."

The sparrow shook its head, squinted, and left a dropping on Pike's sack-clothed shoulder.

"No. It's one quest in two integrally linked parts. Can't do one without the other. And I doubt you could do either."

"Why not?"

"With that skin condition? You'd never survive the acidic vapours of the Stinking Peat Bogs of Lanklandishire, and even if you did, there's a fair maiden who would really want to stay put if she saw you coming at her. Yikes, she'd probably dive in even deeper."

"I can't believe I'm sitting on a pointy stone, being crapped on and insulted by a talking sparrow!"

"And I," said the stone, "can't believe I'm trapped in here, being sat on by a rancid fish-faced youth who's being crapped on and insulted by a sparrow."

The sparrow raised an eye. "You know, that stone sounds exactly like Moorlock the Warlock – apart, that is, from the fact of being muffled by your scrawny rump."

"It is me, sparrow; and as if my eternal damnation were not enough, this youth has passed wind."

"It's the shock!" snapped Pike.

"Sire," said the sparrow, "it's useless. This Pike is not suited to the mission. We need a replacement."

"It's too late for that," whined the stone. "The die is cast and the youth must fulfil his destiny. He must act immediately, so send him on his way. And for the love of Herne, give him some moisturiser, pur-leaze!".

2: PREPARATION

"What we need," said the sparrow, shuffling around the back of Pike's neck, "is some supplies, so we don't starve. I'm rather partial to fresh millet, myself. We need all-weather clothing, some strong leather bags, and something for you to ride on: a trusty steed. I can fly, but your legs look like they'd break after half a mile of hiking over rugged terrain."

"You could try a compliment, instead," sniffed Pike, walking away from the stone circle and back towards Ooze. "You do know that insults are no way to encourage a workforce, don't you?"

The sparrow jumped in the air, flying alongside Pike's right ear. "What are you, some kind of motivational guru?"

"No, but if I was I'd be better at it than you." He whisked a fly off his nose, dislodging yet more flakes of skin. "If you must know, Molag the Melon Mogul was training me to help with this year's harvest. He told me a thing or two about getting the best out of a work-force. Shall I take you to him? You might learn something."

"Not on your life," replied the little bird, landing on Pike's head and digging its claws in as hard as it could, making him grimace. "All I need to know is how to get you out of this good-for-nothing place and on the road to your glorious destiny. Now, if you could just figure out where the nearest skin specialist lives, we'd have a head start on that glorious bit I mentioned."

Pike stopped sharply and jerked his head back, causing the bird to slide down his greasy hair and dangle upside down before his eyes.

"Enough of the insults! Any more and I'll spit roast you over the camp fire for supper."

The sparrow let go and landed the right way up on the grass in front of Pike.

"Well! That, actually, isn't very motivational at all, so I think that your mad Molag the Melon Mogul man has failed you. All this 'New Age of the New

Dawn' stuff drives me crazy. You'll be trying meditation, next."

They reached the hamlet. It was not a pretty sight. Once again, the butcher's stall had been trashed by the wayward horse. However, this time, the fruit-seller had had the foresight to put wheels on his stall and was currently being chased around the village meadow by the large, piebald stallion. The stall-holder weaved from side to side, causing the fruit to spill over the edge of his cart; as fast as it landed it was mercilessly trampled by the beast, which seemed to luxuriate in the squishing of it. This didn't seem to matter to the wizened old man who was pushing the cart as fast as he could: it just appeared to be a matter of principle to him that the horse did not belly-flop onto his display.

Pike stopped to observe the scene. The sparrow parked itself on his head.

"Interesting animal," commented the bird. "Looks like the best fed creature in the village."

The bird was right. Pike looked at the straggle of villagers and for the first time he noticed just how scrawny they were. Out of the twenty or so there, only one could have been classed as mildly portly – and then only because she was six-months pregnant. The rest might have been skeletons with tight-fitting body stockings for skin.

"That's probably because every day that horse smashes up the market and no one buys the stuff afterwards."

"Sounds tragic. What does everyone eat, then?"

"Some of the men go out hunting. They catch the occasional toad or rabbit. Sometimes field mice, or a tasty rat. Just the other day we had a real feast when old man Lallicray brought back a brace of wild sparrow and—"

The bird shot down the front of Pike's sackcloth clothing and stuck its beak out just enough to say, "Sparrow? You ate sparrow? Cannibal!"

"Ah, sorry. Shouldn't have mentioned it. Actually, it wasn't sparrow; it was a brace of wild, wild, erm, wild, er-er … Skylark! Yep. That was it. Skylark."

The sparrow's head popped out.

"Skylark, eh? You sure?"

"Yep," lied Pike.

The sparrow flew out, landing on his shoulder. "So who owns that magnificent stallion, then?"

Pike glared at the tiny bird, or he would have, if it hadn't been so close to his ear that he could barely see it. "Don't you know anything? No one owns horses: they are 'of the land'."

He watched the bizarre chase until both stall and horse disappeared behind a row of rickety houses. Haughtily, he continued, "They are the sacred beasts of legend. Grand, noble and honourable creatures, who serve no one but themselves – and they only have to do that on holy days, when everyone's down at the stone circles, carrying out ritualistic sacrifices and making offerings to the Gods. That is not a beast of burden, like a sheep or a hound; that is the finest example of the work of the great goddess Equinnus Quadrupedius. That there is a—"

"FILTHY THIEVIN' MULE!" screamed a shrill, hag-like voice.

"Couldn't have put it better myself," said the sparrow.

Pike was horrified. "That's my Gran," he yelled, running off towards the houses. "Blaspheming bitch!"

About half of Gran's thatching lay on the rutted track outside her front door. About a quarter of it remained near the apex of the roof. The other quarter was being dragged across the meadow by a hungry horse. Pike and Gran surveyed the damage, standing inside the house, which was now little different from standing on the outside.

"Look at 'im, Pike," wailed Gran. "An 'oss, eatin' me out of 'ouse an' 'ome. It's not roight."

"Look on the bright side, Gran," consoled Pike. "The gods have chosen you. This is truly a great honour."

"Gods? Chosen? Me? You stupid boy! This aren't no gods' work: that 'oss is a demon. May it rot in 'ell." She stamped her foot, glowering at him.

"You'll be rotting in hell, if you talk like that about the noble beast."

"Don't you talk loike that t'ya dear ol' Gran, my lad. And why 'ave ee got a bird behind your ear?"

In all the turmoil, Pike had forgotten his new-found irritant. The little creature hopped out from behind his left ear and sat on his shoulder, making sparrow-like noises.

"Ah, yeah … we just met. This is a sparrow."

"Oi can see that, yoom idiot doom-brain. Wot's ee doing there, on that shoulder? Brought him 'ome to Gran for 'er supper, 'ave ee?" Her tone softened. "Now, now, there's a noice lil birdie. Come to Gran, come on."

She reached out her right hand, rubbing her thumb and forefinger together as if she might be concealing a tasty morsel of sparrow food between them. Her lips pursed. She let out a high-pitched twittering sound, hurting Pike's ear drums.

"Thur-thur, moy lil 'un. Come on, come on, c—AAARRRGHHH!"

The sparrow leapt from Pike's shoulder, screeching on top of its voice, attacking her dry, crusted hand. Its beak and claws ripped her skin with gusto.

"I'm nobody's supper, you old witch," shrieked the bird, between mouthfuls of finger flesh.

"Sparrow! Stop eating Gran. Stop eating her," shouted Pike, trying to prise the bird away, amidst the screaming and the flapping.

"Eat or be eaten," shouted the sparrow, diving in for another bite.

"Gerimoff! Gerimoff! It 'urts!" screamed Gran.

Surprised by the strength of the bird, Pike managed to wrench the screaming creature away, enclosing it between his cupped hands.

"Lemme at her," shrieked the bird.

"Calm down," urged Pike.

"Calm down? That bird tried to eat me," she wailed.

"It's sensitive. It—" Pike was interrupted by the bird's protestations and threats. "Shut up, sparrow."

"Sensitive? Ee's a sparrow. 'Ow can ee be sensitive. Look at moy 'and. Arf eaten."

Pike had to agree that her hand had looked better.

"It doesn't like people talking about eating him, that's all. You wouldn't, either."

"It's a bird, doom-brain. 'Ow would it know?"

"Because it talks. Can't you hear? It hasn't stopped jabbering since you tried to get it off my shoulder."

"All Oi can 'ear is ee scritchin at me."

"The stupid old biddy can't understand me, Pike. Only you can. If I wanted to I could call her a crusty old piece of sh—"

"That's enough, sparrow," Pike chided. "I'll be offended, even if she isn't."

Gran took a step backwards.

"Yoom talkin' to a bird: yoom talkin' to a bird. That's not roight. Yoom not roight in the 'ead, boy."

"And so say all of us," said Pike. "Not only am I talking to it, but it's talking to me, in English. It says only I can understand it. I have a mission."

Gran dropped to her knees, clutching her heart, wailing. "Yoom wuz moy favourite, and yoom lost your moind! Gods have mercy on 'im."

"Gran, I'm not mad, it was Moorlock who gave me the mission. The sparrow is here to guide me."

"Moorlock? That charlatan?"

"No, he's a warlock. Maybe he's a charlatan in his spare time … you know, as a hobby."

"Fish face," the sparrow intervened, "can you stop this crazy talk with the old bat and get on with matters at hand? We need to leave before nightfall, and you've got a horse to catch."

Pike started to reply, despite haranguing from the old woman. "I told you, damned bird, that horse is a noble beast, a gift from the gods, didn't I? I can't just go out and catch it."

Gran stopped her diatribe and grinned.

"Pike, moy love. Are ee sayin' that sparrow wants ee to catch the old nag?"

"That's what it's saying, Gran."

"Hmm," she smiled. "Maybe ee's got more sense'n you, after all."
Sparrow chipped in with: "And then learn to ride it."
"Sings noice, dun ee?" said Gran.

Catching the horse was easier than Pike anticipated. It merely required him to drag the half of the thatched roof from the dirt track to the back of Gran's house and to whistle loudly in the horse's general direction. The hardest part was listening to the old crone yelling at him to leave her roof alone.

"'Ow's Oi s'posed to sleep in moy own 'ome with no roof on it?" she pleaded.

"Sleep at mum's house," said Pike, gently stroking the horse's rump, as it chewed at the roofing thatch. "Looks like my bed'll be spare tonight. One of my brothers can fix this in the morning."

"So that's it, is it? Off you go, on nothing' more'n the say-so of a sparrow."

"And a warlock, don't forget."

"Ah, 'im." She tapped her right foot on the hardened soil, looking down with a distant expression on her face.

The sparrow, who had been sitting between the horse's ears, twittering away at great speed, flew over to Pike's shoulder.

"What's she got against Moorlock?" asked the bird.

"Don't know. Ask her."

"Yeah, right," shrugged the sparrow. "She understands the language of sparrows perfectly well, as you've seen."

"Good point," huffed Pike. "Gran, what have you got against Moorlock?"

"I ain't got nuthin' agin 'im. Nope, Nuthin'. Never did. Never touched 'im. Wouldn't, even if ee wuz the last man on the planet."

It all came out too quickly. Gran turned full circle and wandered back into her open topped home. "Barely know 'im. Wouldn't loike 'im if Oi did, I'm sure."

"Strange reaction," commented the sparrow, as she disappeared inside.

"Very," agreed Pike.

"Wouldn't touch 'im with a ten-adult-foot pole, Oi wouldn't," called Gran, hidden from view. Suddenly she reappeared at the back door. "In fact, Oi'll bet ee's covered in bruises, where folk 'ave fended 'im off with long poles, tryin' not to touch 'im with 'em! So there!"

3: SETTING OUT

The air, heavy with smoke from a cooking fire, stung Pike's eyes as he entered his mother's house. The smell of soup bones combined with the odour of hot, cramped bodies. Around a dozen people, mainly male, occupied the one downstairs room; they united in ignoring him, murmuring and chuckling as they slurped down their broth from leather tankards. By the light of the fire and a flickering lantern, Pike could see his mother sitting in the midst of the men; she was minus the watermelon skin hat and her lank hair appeared glued to her dirty forehead. Pike coughed loudly and deliberately.

And then again.

After two minutes of still being ignored, he tried a new approach. "I'm going on a quest, mother," he announced.

"Have some broth before you go, there's a good lad."

His mother turned back to one of the older men and carried on a conversation Pike hadn't noticed they were having.

"I am going on the orders of Moorlock the Warlock. It's my destiny."

This caught her attention. She stood up from the group and walked over to face her son. Several of the men cursed as she trod on various body parts.

"You're Pike. You don't have a destiny."

"Do! Moorlock told me so. I'm the seventh son of a seventh son, so it must be true." Pike folded his arms, feeling a little self satisfied. She couldn't argue with that logic.

"Pah!" she spat, her rancid breath jettisoning towards Pike, awakening a feeling of nausea within him. "You're the fifth son of the first out of fifteen sons and most your brothers are dead."

He quickly unfolded his arms.

"Dead? Who are this lot, then?"

"Uncles mostly, cousins, some, and I don't know who that is," she said, looking curiously at a small hunch-backed character with a wart on the end of his nose, who sat on the periphery of the group. The hunch-back smiled, waved and left rapidly.

"Are you sure? Is it true?"

His mother sighed. "Yes. And again yes. Your father was the eldest of the boys. Some of the lads you thought were your brothers were your uncles, but the ages were so similar we didn't think it needed to be told. Your Gran had her hands full so some of them grew up with you. So that obviously puts the mockers on your quest, I'd say."

Pike slumped to the floor, not yet having absorbed the story.

"Soup?"

"Soup? You offer me soup at a time like this? You must be wrong. This is my quest: I've got the chance to make something of myself, and you just want to ruin it for me."

She turned to the remaining men. "Bless him, he's got ambitions, just like his father – and see where that got him." This raised a laugh or two from the older ones. She turned back to her scaly faced son. "I'm not wrong, my lad. Your dad was Aradrick. Then there was Baradrick, Caradrick, Daradrick, Earadrick, Faradrick, Garadrick, Haradrick, Iaradrick, Jaradrick, Karadrick, Laradrick, Maradrick, Naradrick and ... oh, what was his name? ... ah yes. Bert. Always have trouble remembering that one. There were some sisters, but they're not important.

"Your old Gran used to rule that family with an iron fist. She'd have them out in the fields, morning till nightfall. She'd call them in from time to time, just to make sure none had gone missing."

"How come the last one was called Bert?" asked Pike.

"Well, it got confusing for your Gran. She'd be calling them in, randomly. 'Caradrick' she'd call, meaning the one spelled with a 'c', and along would come Karadrick with a 'k'. He'd get a whack across the head for not listening. Then there was Baradrick and Daradrick: when she shouted them out no one could tell the difference. One day she called out for Daradrick and along came Baradrick. 'What are you doing here?' she yells at him. 'I wanted Daradrick.' And Baradrick goes all wimpish and cries and says, 'He's dead. He died in my arms just yesterday. Don't you remember, mother?' And your poor old Gran just didn't know what to do with herself. Laugh? Ah, the whole village laughed right along with her. Them was good old times."

"I'm not listening to this, mother: you're just trying to stop me from going, and you can't. I'm going out the back for my tool bag, and then I'm off."

His mother's expression changed from one of nostalgic smugness to that of a concerned parent. It wasn't an expression Pike recognised, so he thought she was about to turn nasty. He was surprised when she said: "Pike, my little fish. The world's a big dangerous place. Lots of evil people would be waiting to take advantage of a boy like you. And just outside of Ooze is the estate of

Lord du Well. If you go wandering onto his land he'll have you quartered for poaching, soon as look at you."

"I don't see why he'd do that to me, just for cooking eggs," said Pike, wondering if she had finally gone as mad as his Gran.

She ignored his remark. "Evil thugs: evil. It's not a safe place for a boy to set out alone."

"I won't be alone. I will be accompanied by a trusty sparrow and a noble steed. I'll be safe."

A look of horror gripped her face. "A steed? You mean a horse?"

Pike nodded.

"Cursed! Cursed, I tell you!"

She backed off hesitantly toward the assembled men. They murmured their disapproval.

"Only a demon could tame such a beast. My son, a demon!" She crumpled to the ground, kneeling on the straw, swaying back and forth. "He was my tiddler, now he's a demon. May the gods spare him."

The men murmured something sounding vaguely like "Demon fish," and several reached out to comfort the sobbing woman.

"Right. Well. I'll get my stuff and be off then. Bye."

He left quickly via the back door, collected his tool bag from behind the water butt and walked around the outside of the house to meet up with the sparrow and the horse.

After the smoky, soupy humidity of the house, the night air felt chilly. He shuddered as he placed the tool bag on the ground. The sparrow stirred from between the horse's ears.

"Got everything?"

"I got my tool bag."

"That's not everything."

"'Tis to me. I haven't got anything else."

"So all that stuff I said about decent walking boots, cold weather clothing, wet weather clothing, decent baggage et cetera, et cetera: it just washed over you, did it?"

"This is Ooze, not some rich place. What I wear is all I own, apart from my tools. And I could do without being told off by a sparrow. Anyway, what is your name? I can't keep calling you sparrow."

The little bird fluttered over to Pike's shoulder. "Thought you'd never ask. Fynch: Robyn Fynch."

Pike guffawed. "You are joking, aren't you?"

Robyn flew back to the horse, indignantly. "Why would I be?"

"They're both types of bird."

"Pike, you are an incomplete idiot. I doubt we'll ride out from this village without meeting our sorry deaths at the hands of an earth worm. Not Robin and Finch with 'I': they both have a 'y'. By Hearne, you are a daft one. I mean, if I was named Robyn with an 'i' that would mean I would either be a red-breasted bird of low IQ or a boy with an effeminate name, and I'm neither."

"So you're a girl, then?"

"Yes I am."

"Don't sound like a girl."

"I sound like a girl sparrow, but you wouldn't know the difference, It's all just twittering to you humans."

"But your voice: it's like a man."

"You hear me in your head, you numbskull. The voice you hear is your interpretation of what you thought I was. Hell, you didn't think I could really talk, did you? A talking sparrow? Whatever next?"

"Try a talking horse," said the horse in a low, wavering baritone.

This was almost too much for Pike. He stomped to the horse and looked it in the eye: no mean feat in the darkness.

"Boy or girl?" demanded Pike.

"Stallion: you figure it out."

"Just checking. Name?"

The horse let out a shrill noise that dwindled off into a throaty wheeze and a snotty snort. "That's what my friends call me, at any rate. There's no translation that you would understand, so you may call me Horse. No, better still: MISTER Horse. It might help you with the gender confusion."

While Pike steadied himself from the shock, Robyn said, "Time to go. We need to be far into du Well's estate by sun up, or we'll probably be captured and eaten alive."

"OK," said Pike. "But I'm not riding this sacred beast."

"Then you're an idiot," said the sacred beast.

"And I'll not be insulted by it."

"Pathetic fool."

Pike walked by the side of the great beast with Robyn sitting on his shoulder. Her voice had become more feminine, now that Pike was aware she was a girl. "We'll need to sort out provisions on the journey. I was hoping you'd have brought stuff from home. There's some rough land to cross in the coming weeks."

Pike shrugged. "This is all a huge mistake. I'll die, you'll fly away and find a new champion, Mr Horse will ascend to a higher plain … Here, what you said earlier, about dying at the hands of an earthworm: they don't have hands."

"You think not?"

"I think not."

"Then you obviously associate with a lesser class of earthworm."

"Like I said," Horse whinnied, "pathetic fool."

*

The trio approached the woods. It was a clear night and the almost full moon cast long shadows. This was not a problem outside of the tree line, but once inside, all the long shadows mingled into one large black blob. Robyn flew away, she said, to see what lay ahead.

"Ouch!"

"What's wrong?" asked an alarmed Pike.

Robyn landed close to his left ear, whimpering. She rubbed her right eye with a wing. "This is why I don't do night flights: it's unnatural, unless you're an owl."

Pike reached up and stroked her head gently. "Are you going to be all right?"

"Yes, of course," she said, pulling away from his fingertips. "None of that soppy, pally stuff. I'm not a pet. This is strictly business."

"So what lies ahead then?"

"Trees. Very large trees."

Horse, who had fallen behind slightly, drew to a sudden halt at Pike's side, sniffing the air. His head bobbed up and down. "I smell water."

"Yep," said Pike. "Ooze."

Horse rested his chin on Pike's right shoulder. "I dunno. Whose d'you suppose?"

"No: Ooze. The River Ooze."

"Right. Do we cross it?"

"We turn right and keep going till first light," answered Robyn, "then we cross it. If we try in the dark you'll drown, Horse."

"What about me? Horse is much more likely to survive the river than me."

"Sorry. I thought you'd look more at home in the water."

Pike decided to ignore the little bird's comment, even though he was tiring of the constant insults.

Within minutes they reached the water's edge. The river was much narrower than the area Pike normally visited, but it was still too wide to cross safely. It flowed more rapidly than at any part of it he had previously seen. In the lunar glow, the water was tipped silvery white as it rushed over rocks and boulders.

They followed Robyn's instruction and walked alongside the torrent. Pike decided he ought to say something before it was too late.

"I think Moorlock was wrong to choose me."

Horse started to say something, but spluttered instead.

"Why so?" Robyn asked.

"Because I remember all those years ago, when I first saw him, he asked me if I was the seventh son of a seventh son, and I think I told him I was. But I'm not."

"And that's important because …?"

"Because after that he said he thought I was the one, and he told me to meet him back at the stone when I was sixteen. If I hadn't told him I was the seventh son of a seventh son he wouldn't have believed I was the one."

"Really? Oh well, we'll just turn back and abandon the whole idea, then."

"Good. I'm not the quest sort of person, really. Rather be at home in bed. Ow!"

Robyn had pecked his ear lobe suddenly. "Not the quest sort of person? Rather be at home in bed? People's lives are at stake here, and you want to go sleepy-byes? We should just throw you in the water and leave you there."

Pike stopped. So did Horse, who was remaining tactfully silent.

"It's no use me doing this, is it? I'm an embarrassment to both of you and I'm not the right one. I'm sure there's a seventh-seventh thingy nearby who can do it."

Robyn flew round to Pike's nose and landed on it, gripping tightly with her sharp little claws.

"Ow, gerroff!"

"No. Not until you've listened to me. You have been chosen: hand selected. All that crap about seventh son of a seventh son is exactly that: crap. It's just the stuff that warlocks and people like that talk about. Maybe if you were one you'd have more luck and a better complexion, but the fact is, you were the one on the stone that day, and it is you who has been chosen, despite your mongrelistic genealogy."

"My what?"

"Never mind. Just remember that you have a job to do, and so do I. My job is to make sure you do yours."

"And what's Horse's job?"

"I can look pretty," said Horse, flatly.

"He's your steed – or he would be, if you'd ever get on his back and ride him."

"I'd rather just look pretty."

"Horse. You are a chosen horse: one that has been selected to aid this noble Pike in his quest. You can look pretty with him on your back."

"You want him on me?"

"Yes."

"Like a pimple."

"No. Like a valiant hero."

"A hero, eh?" inquired Horse, taking a deep breath. "I need time to consider. I will consult my ancestors."

Horse walked a few paces away to a large tree, possibly an oak (it was impossible to tell in the darkness). He faced the trunk, bobbed his neck up and down a few times, and then banged his forehead hard against it. He remained there, his head pressed against the bark.

"What's he doing," asked Pike.

"Consulting his ancestors."

Several minutes passed slowly by, during which time Horse could be heard to huff and blow out through his nose and mouth, rattling his lips. Pike also thought he could hear him take the occasional nibble at the low level greenery that sprouted from the base of the tree. Eventually, the huge, piebald stallion turned to face them and trod slowly back to Pike and Robyn.

"My ancestors were most helpful. Maybe this will be good for me and my kind. Man and sacred beast, working in harmony. Together we could defeat all our foes."

"That's more like it," interjected Robyn, gleefully rubbing her wing tips together and nearly blinding Pike in the process.

"We shall ride day and night, oblivious to the dangers that lurk around every bend."

"Good-ho!"

"Not even the Stinking Peat Bogs of Lanklandishire shall deter us from our quest. All others will fall in our wake. Freshly emerging butterflies will invert themselves back into their cocoons at the very sound of our names. My hoof beats, heavy with the weight of the rider on my back, shall herald the new age of chivalry. Earthworms shall retreat at our sight, clasping their tiny hands over their eyes. Together we shall reign supreme. No one shall stand in our—"

"Yes, yes, very good. Now shut up. Pike, get on his back."

"Only if you get off my nose."

"Point taken."

Robyn landed on a low branch next to Horse's head.

"OK. How'd you get on his back?" asked Pike.

"Well, normally I'd fly, but from here I could hop."

Pike huffed. "Not you, me! How do I get on his back?"

"Hmm, that could be tricky."

"Yep. Never thought of that," said Horse. "I suppose you could try climbing a tree and getting on to me from up there."

Pike scratched his chin; flakes of skin dropped to the forest floor, like small moonlit snowflakes.

"That's OK for now, but what about when we're in the open, with no trees around?"

"You could run and vault onto me."

"OK. Let's try the tree, first. That one looks sturdy enough."

It wasn't easy, climbing an unchartered tree by night, but after a few minutes Pike was high enough to slide across onto Horse's back. Robyn flew over to him.

"Remember to be very gentle at first. I doubt anyone's ever climbed on to Horse's back before."

Pike shuddered at the thought of being the first ever human to desecrate a sacred horse by riding it.

"No. I can't do it."

"Don't be silly. He's invited you to ride him. It's not a sin."

"But it doesn't feel right: it's not right."

"I'm the horse around here, and I say it's all right." Without a hint of sarcasm, Horse continued, "Climb aboard, heroic but flaky one."

Slowly, carefully, Pike slid across onto Horse's back. Horse stirred beneath him.

"I think you're too close to the front," he said.

Pike slid back into the dip of Horse's back.

"Is that OK?"

"Hmm, feels odd. New. Unusual. I think I need to walk around a bit. Hold on to my mane."

Horse took a few faltering steps. Pike slid from side to side and clutched on to the mane, trying not to fall off.

Horse said, "I think I'll get used to it, but—"

"Me too," interrupted Pike, less sure than he sounded.

Horse continued, "—but for now, I feel I need … erm … ahhh … oh no, this isn't good. I need to, need to WOAWHOAHHH!"

Horse bucked violently, rearing up on his hind legs, throwing Pike into the trees. Pike's head struck a trunk with a loud thunk.

"Sorry."

Pike did not respond. Robyn flapped over to the youth, landing on his chest.

"Pike? Pike? PIKE!"

Pike grunted.

"What the hell was that about, Horse? You trying to kill him?"

"I said I was sorry, didn't I? I couldn't stop myself. My ancestors warned me that I may have to be broken in gently before anyone can ride me."

"Great. You've knocked him senseless and he can't even ride on you."

"I'm all right," mumbled Pike, drunkenly. "I can walk. If I can stand, that is."

Horse cautiously walked towards him.

"I really am sorry, Pike. I didn't mean to do it. I'm not sure what came over me. Here, hold my muzzle; I'll help you up."

Pike reached up and took hold of either side of Horse's long face. Horse backed away slowly, raising the lad as he did so. Until Pike's hands slipped and he tumbled back to the ground.

"Oops. Sorry again."

Horse backed off quickly this time, sniffed the ground around the base of a tree, and went back, dropping a sturdy stick at Pike's feet.

"You take hold of the stick at one end, I'll bite onto the other and pull you up. Ready?"

This time it worked well, save for the splinters in Pike's fingers. Pike stood and leant against Horse's warm body.

"I feel sick and dizzy, and I think my head is bleeding," he sighed, his voice muffled by Horse's lush hide.

Robyn landed on his head.

"Yes. That's blood, all right."

"I feel really bad about this," said Horse.

"Me too," sobbed Pike.

"You shouldn't try to walk in that condition. I think you should try and ride me again. It'll be OK this time. Look: it's starting to get light. I can see a raised bank over there." He nodded his head in the direction they were headed. Sure enough, Pike could see that the path split in two, with one rising quite high above the other. "Try walking that far, then you take the high road, and I'll take the low road, and you should be able to get on me from there. Hey, that reminds me of a song I once heard."

Ten minutes later, much against his better judgement, Pike found himself sitting on the edge of the raised path, ready to slide over onto Horse's back. Horse positioned himself and took several long, deep breaths.

"Ommmmmmmmmm. Ommmmmmmmm."

"What the heck is that supposed to be?" squawked Robyn, who was fluttering around Horse's head.

"It's an ancient meditative technique. It dates back to a long forgotten epoch, when mystical moorland ponies roamed the Earth, and especially the Moor of Dart. I'm calming myself in preparation for a rider. Ommmmmmmmmm. Ommmmmmmmm."

"Finished?"

"Ommmmmmmmmm. Ommmmmmmmm. Now I've finished."

"Good," said Robyn. "Prepare yourself, Pike. It's now or never. Ready?"

Pike nodded. The pain in his head reminded him that he shouldn't have.

"Right. Get on his back, then."

Pike slid across carefully, positioning himself in the dip, like before. Horse continued to take deep breaths, releasing the occasional ommmmmmmmmm between clenched teeth. When Pike was settled, Horse stepped forward a few paces.

"Yey. That feels better. I could get used to this. Look at me, everybody: I have a rider. This could start a new trend."

He carried on walking, slowly.

"You know, Pike, it's as if we were meant to be together, you and I. This must be part of our joint destinies. We each have our own to fulfil, of course, but for the time being our paths have crossed and we must assist one another in this quest. The gods are smiling on us, I can feel it. It's like, like, it's like … arghhhhhhh WOAWHOAHHH!"

There was a thud when Pike hit the ground, winded.
"Hmm, sorry 'bout that. Would you like to try again?"

4: HE'LL DU WELL

The sun had fully risen by the time the unlikely trio left the forest. Pike's rejection of his mother's broth now seemed foolish in the extreme, as he had not eaten since the previous lunchtime. After a few more false starts and bruisings, he was glad to be riding on Horse's back; in his hungry and weakened state he would probably have fallen over if he had to walk. The pain in his head subsided a little once the throbbing synchronised itself with Horse's hoof beats, and he was reluctant to ask the beast to stop, even though hunger was stabbing at his belly like a hot poker. However, Pike was well aware that if he didn't eat soon he would not make it through the day.

Through heavily lidded eyes he looked around and slowly came to terms with his surroundings. Gone was the dense woodland. It had been replaced with more openness, although there was no shortage of trees and bushes. The land was reasonably flat, but seemed to rise into mountainous terrain off towards the horizon. The early morning aromas of pollen and greenery were almost overpowering and somehow emphasised his hunger. The River Ooze still flowed to their left, Robyn having now decreed that they should get well away from the forest and to much calmer waters before attempting to cross.

"Horse, we need to stop. I have to eat," moaned Pike, unable to control himself any longer.

"Sad thing, really," said Horse. "I was getting used to this. There's some nice lush grass over there. That should satisfy your hunger."

Robyn, who had been resting between Horse's ears, said, "I don't think Pike's eat grass. He'll probably need a rabbit, or something."

Horse jerked to a halt.

"Rabbit? He eats rabbits?"

"I would, if I had one to eat," yawned Pike.

Horse snorted, turning his head to look back at his rider.

"I, too, like rabbits. I don't think I'm happy with the idea of my noble and esteemed rider murdering my friends and eating them. My best friend used to be a rabbit."

"Well that's OK, because I'm hardly likely to catch one out here, am I? There's you, me, a sparrow and a bag of rusty tools. I'll be eating leaves before I catch a rabbit. Anyway, what do you mean, your best friend used to be a rabbit? What is he now?"

"Rabbit stew: devoured, digested, excreted."

Pike looked quizzically at Robyn for a translation.

"He means in one end, out the other."

"Ah," said Pike. "I'm hardly likely to get that opportunity, am I?"

Still not moving, Horse said, "Let's get this right: you won't be eating a rabbit because you won't be able to catch one, but in actual fact you have no objection to the overall principle?"

"That's about it. Right now I would eat anything put in front of me. By the Gods, I swear I'm so hungry I could eat a HHHHORSSSSSSE!"

Pike landed on his back. Horse swung around and threateningly plonked a fore-hoof on Pike's chest, pinning him to the ground and staring him in the eye.

"You are not my friend, oh fishy one. You shall ride on my back no more. I shall accompany you on this journey merely as an observer, in the hope that you fail miserably and are eaten alive by the one-eyed winglekrats of the Outer Grenstead Mud Flats."

Pike raised his head a little and rubbed the back of it. Thankfully the wound had not reopened. Then he wondered what a one-eyed winglekrat could be.

"It was just a figure of speech. I didn't really mean I would eat a horse."

"Maybe not. But you would eat my friend the rabbit, and that's as bad."

Robyn kept a cautious distance, watching silently from a nearby bush.

"Sorry, Horse, but I'm a human, and that's what we do."

Horse pushed his snout up against Pike's own nose and huffed.

"I know what humans do. It was humans who once destroyed most of this sorry world."

Pike was startled, but before he could pursue it, Robyn landed next to them and said, "Leave it, Horse. You can't blame him for what is passed. He's an innocent."

Horse snorted again, covering Pike with horse snot.

"They're all innocent, every last, evil one of them."

He walked away to a clearing in the trees and started to graze. Pike lay still for a while, considering what had been said. He gradually became aware of a warm, soggy feeling under his back, and wondered what it could be. Robyn bounced onto his chest.

"Do you think you can get up?"

"I think I can."

"You need to get food and we need to get moving before du Well's guards find us here. We're well into his territory, and he's madly protective of it. We should have been near the other boundary by now."

"What did Horse mean, about destroying the world?"

"Forget it. It's just a story from the collective consciousness of horses. Now, sit up gradually. I don't want you fainting."

"OK, but as I'm getting up, can you just look behind me and see what I've landed in? I hope it's not dung."

The sparrow jumped off Pike's chest and landed on a twig on the ground. Pike slowly started to rise, but found it hard. His head throbbed, his joints ached, and his knees felt like they had been forced apart by a large canoe placed lengthways between them. Surely he'd never stand straight-legged again? Even his toes ached. He must have made some noise as he tried to get up, as Horse looked over and gave him the evil eye.

"That's good," said Robyn. "Keep moving, you'll make it."

Horse began to approach them slowly, and Robyn carried on with the encouraging noises.

"OK, Pike, I can see something under the small of your back. Just a little bit further, that's it … a bit more … yep, that's a good fellow. Ackkk! LIE DOWN!"

Pike dropped back on command, fearing the worst. Maybe he'd landed on a sharp stick, and the warmth was his blood, soaking through his sack-cloth garment.

"What is it? Is it bad?"

Horse drew nearer.

Robyn shuddered. "It's worse than bad. This is really serious."

"Holy Hearne. Will I die?"

"You will if I don't act fast. Wait here."

Robyn flew off rapidly, landing on Horse's head. After an exchange that Pike could not hear, Horse turned and walked away. Robyn flew back. Pike felt very sad: his one time out of the hamlet of Ooze and he was going to die after being unceremoniously dumped by a noble and blessed beast. He knew it was too much, to ride on horseback, putting himself on a par with the gods, and now they had scorned him.

Robyn spoke quietly.

"OK Pike, you are going to have to get up very slowly, and don't under any circumstances let Horse see what's behind you."

"Will he feel guilty, causing a death, seeing the injury?"

"Oh, I should say so."

"But why should I get up, if I'm going to die?"

"You'll only die if Horse sees what's under you."

"I think I'd rather stay here and bleed to death peacefully."

"Eh?"

"Well I've obviously got a fatal injury."

"Not so much."

"So what did I land on, then?"

"You've landed on a …"

"Ye-es?"

"On a …"

"Get on with it, sparrow."

"A …"

"A what?"

"A rabbit."

"You mean … ?"

"Yes, I mean. Horse threw you off, you squished a rabbit, he's going to kill you if he finds out."

Pike sat up straight, suddenly.

"This is great news. I get to eat fresh rabbit."

"Not if you're dead."

"Oh, come on. He can't get mad over this. I didn't ask to be thrown off. I didn't intentionally kill the little bunny." He reached behind him and picked up the still warm and twitching corpse.

"Think it'll be all right, crushed like this?"

"Put it down. He'll see you."

"Could I eat it raw?"

"You can't eat it at all. Horse will trample you to death."

Pike brought the rabbit up to his mouth and tried to tear the flesh around its neck with his teeth.

"Pah, splah, ugghhh! Th'tuh,th'tuh. Gross! Gor fur thstuck in my th'teeth. Th'tuh, th'tuh. Splah!"

"Pike: you're an idiot. He's heard you."

Horse was indeed staring curiously in their direction, as if he might at any moment form a one-horse stampede. Perhaps, had it not been for the strange noises coming from the bushes, he may have done. Pike looked along the path they had followed, but could see nothing. He looked the other way and saw a blur of movement in the undergrowth. He heard strange 'Ma'aa, ma'aaaa," noises, accompanied by the sound of pounding feet and the jangling of something metallic. It seemed that Horse also heard, as his attention was diverted towards the din.

"What is that?" asked Pike.

"I think," said Robyn, "we're about to be captured by du Well's men."

Suddenly, something burst through the bushes. It was like nothing Pike had ever seen. A tall, lean man, wearing a silvery, metal suit and carrying a long, crooked stick was closely followed by a team of sixteen sheep. The sheep were harnessed in four rows of four, the front row being linked by a single central harness to the man. Behind the sheep was a black and gold, open topped carriage. Its wheels were half the height of Pike. Sitting within the carriage was a young man, dressed all in black, complete with a bicorn hat worn so that the points protruded to the front and back. His collar-length hair was brown, soft and wavy. Although he was young, he displayed a full-set beard and moustache. Alongside the carriage jogged a dozen men, six on either side. They were also dressed in metal suits and all looked the wrong side of tired to continue for much longer.

"Muth! Muth!" called the man in the carriage, using a lengthy rod to whip and prod the leading man. Then, on seeing Pike, he called, "Halt."

The leading man stopped and the sheep did as well, but only after they ran into him, pushing him over. Amidst the "Baaas" and "Maaas" came the cursing of the metal clad man and the screech of the carriage being brought to a halt by its rider applying the lever-brake to the steel-rimmed wheels.

The bearded passenger looked around in apparent dismay at the dozen other men alongside his carriage. He spoke: "Perhapth a few of you good tholes could athitht the thsephard to hith feet."

The men mumbled and murmured and went to help, rattling as they moved.

Pike looked around at Robyn and whispered: "What is that?"

"It's the Lord du Well in a sheep drawn buggy."

"I've heard of them, but I've never seen one. What about the man up front?"

"He will be the shepherd."

"Why's he there?"

"Because, sheep being sheep, they will only follow, not lead. Not much good if you want them to pull you around, is it?"

Lord du Well coughed for attention. The armoured men repositioned themselves alongside the carriage, whilst the shepherd rearranged the harnessed sheep into their rows.

"Thsepherd? Who dairths to thit on my thoil?"

"Who dares to sit on the Lord du Well's soil?" boomed the shepherd.

Pike began to stand.

"How dare he thstand without my permithion? Tell him to thit. No! To kneel, and bow before me."

"YOU! Kneel, and bow before—"

"I heard," Pike interrupted. He began to kneel when he realised he was still holding on to the rabbit. Du Well must also have noticed.

"What ith that ugly youth holding in hith handths?" he demanded.

Before the shepherd could relay the message, Pike answered: "Just a dead rabbit. Nothing much."

Du Well raised himself from his seat.

"Did that rabbit die on my land?" he asked commandingly, the effect being ruined with the sneering addition of, "Oh fithshy fathed one?"

"If this is your land, then yes, it did."

"THIETHZE THAT YOUTH!" yelled du Well. "He'th been poaching. I won't thtand for it."

The dozen men advanced and clanged in unison. Pike didn't even try to get away. He was far too hungry to care, right then. Also, he didn't understand what 'thiethze' meant. Before he could react he found that his hands were chained behind his back, and the rabbit had been taken from him.

"Hold on! I've got places to go. You can't do this."

"The only plathe you'll be going ith to prithon, convicted ath a common thief."

Pike was stunned. "What have I stolen?"

"A-hem: a very thmall rabbit, it appearths," replied Du Well, examining the furry bundle that a soldier had just passed to him. "A very thmall, flat rabbit."

"Ah, you noticed the bit about it being flat, eh? I can explain. I didn't steal it, I fell onto it. It was an accident."

"A very thmall, flat rabbit, with human teeth markth on it'th throat." Du Well looked up at Pike. "Come clo'ther," he said, quietly.

Pike lurched to his feet, wondering why Robyn and Horse were being so quiet. Then he noticed that Horse was nowhere to be seen, and Robyn seemed to have hidden in a tree. He thought he could just make out her form in a nearby sycamore, but it could have been any sparrow, he supposed. He walked towards du Well, wondering where this was going to lead, and stopped next to the carriage.

"If I'm not mithtaken," said du Well, paying close attention to Pike's chin, "thothe are bit'ths of rabbit fur around your lipths."

"Er … I was hungry. I didn't actually eat it." As he spoke, he somehow realised that his words sounded inadequate, under the circumstances.

Haughtily, du Well announced: "I detect we have a poacher in our midthst. Guardth: theize that youth. Again!"

5: INCARCERATED

The journey to Fort du Well was exhausting. Pike was tethered to the front of the sheep in place of the shepherd, who seemed grateful for the break – not that it was very restful for him, for he now had to run alongside the carriage with eleven of the armoured men, shouting directions at Pike lest he deviate from the roughly cut track. In the name of symmetry, du Well ordered that the twelfth guard run behind the carriage. The shepherd's calling mainly consisted of, *"Straight on", "Don't deviate"* and *"Carry on, don't stop. No, really, I do mean don't stop. Why are you stopping?"*

When Pike did stop, hunger having got the better of him, he wished he hadn't: du Well prodded him with his long, sharp stick. The effect on Pike was far more profound than it had been on the shepherd, on account of Pike not wearing any protective armour.

When, at last, they reached the fort, Pike was slightly disappointed. He had expected to find a massive, fortified castle, like those of legend, but this was merely a wooden garrison: large, undoubtedly, but wooden nonetheless. There was a very long outer wall, standing three times the height of an adult, and a pair of massive gates, which swung open towards them as they approached, revealing a bustling village-like scene. Dozens of armoured men patrolled the walls, using high platforms on the inside. Masses of women and children stepped back to allow the sheep-drawn vehicle clear passage. From what he could see, Pike guessed there must be at least fifty wooden buildings comprising shops, homesteads and trading posts, and that was just on the main road leading in. Hearne only knew what else lay beyond.

Slowing to a walk, and glad for not being shouted at by the shepherd (or prodded by du Well's stick), Pike saw that they were approaching a large square, which appeared to lie at the centre of the fort. On the far side of it was a building that was much larger and grander than anything he had seen before. This was no shack: it had tall, smooth walls, painted the colour of pink rose petals, and many windows, which all appeared to have some kind of see-through, shiny substance filling in the holes. Wooden shutters adorned the walls on each side of the windows, but these appeared to be there as decoration, rather than to stop the elements. Like the window frames, the shutters were painted red. At the centre of the front wall was an archway: it was entirely blocked by a pair of huge wooden doors, which were also red.

"Halt," called the shepherd.

Close to collapse, Pike was only too pleased to oblige.

The shepherd walked forward and tapped on the large doors three times with his crook. Without the merest hint of a creak, the doors gracefully opened inwards.

"Forward: slowly," called the shepherd.

Pike did as he was bid, passing under the high archway and into the heart of the du Well palace.

He led the sheep to the centre of this inner courtyard, casting a backwards glance at them, wondering how many he would have to eat to sate his hunger. Looking at his surrounds he found it hard to accept that such a large open space could exist within the boundary of a building. The building was four stories high, the lower level mainly having been given over to stables. He couldn't guess at the overall size of the place, but he did know that the Fertility Stone clearing would have been dwarfed by it.

A troop of twenty immaculately clad youths in blue and yellow outfits jogged out from several stable doorways towards the sheep-drawn carriage. They silently and efficiently un-tethered Pike from the sheep, and the sheep from each other and the carriage. The animals baa'd appreciatively as they were led to their accommodation, enticed by handfuls of grass. Pike watched them go, slightly in awe of the efficiency of the troop – one person for each sheep, four to carry the harnesses – and envious of the sheep's food. No one spoke to tell him what to do, so he turned around to see what his captor was doing.

Du Well was still in the carriage and had been joined by four dapper men of advancing years. The men were dressed in finely tailored black jackets, skin-tight three-quarter length matching leggings, and sparkly white socks. Their shoes were black, each bearing a large, silver buckle. Their hair-styles were short and combed close to their scalps, unlike Pike's unruly and filthy mop. They assisted du Well to his feet and brushed the dust off his clothing. The guards and the shepherd were all standing rigidly to attention and sweating profusely. The sight of them made Pike glad that his career in Molag's melon fields was assured.

Once du Well was standing, dusted and polished, he instructed the guards.

"Take thith thad thspethimen of a boy and clean him up. Feed and water him if he needth it. I will thpeak to him oneth he ith refresthed."

*

Pike didn't know how he managed to stay awake for the next few hours. He was extremely tired, hungry (even after being fed stale bread and mouldy cheese, with a side order of warm, tinny-tasting water), and his legs ached from riding Horse and running with sheep.

Considering he was a prisoner, his accommodation was not bad and better than home. There was a well-padded mattress on a raised plinth along one wall, complete with a pillow and blanket; in the corner was fitted a strange wooden seat with a hole cut into it, and below that there was a hole that disappeared into the distance. Water was trapped down there, several adult feet below; he could hear it trickling. Pike feared there was a leak somewhere. He supposed that even places like this must suffer from the weather. Still, it was an odd concept, that seat. He could see no use for it: the hole wasn't even big enough to use as an escape route.

The window, set high in the wall, was barred. Like the ones he had seen from the outside, the holes were filled with that transparent shiny stuff. He reached between the bars to feel it: it was solid, hard, cold and very smooth. It struck Pike that it would cost an awful lot of watermelons to barter for windows like that.

He drained the remains of the water from the metal cup and let out a hunger burp that threatened to bring down the walls of the palace. Within seconds a guard opened a small shutter that was at eye level in the heavily studded, iron door.

"Waz that noise?" grunted the man.

Pike could see his whiskery face and thickset nose, but nothing more.

"My guts," he replied. "Look, I know I'm locked in here, but I really need to … you know … erm … use a bush."

The guard blinked, giving away the fact he did not know what Pike meant.

"I'm a bit desperate, actually. That water's gone straight through me. Must be the lack of food to hold it in."

"Oh! Use a bush. Ha. Very clever. Must remember that one. Right. OK."

"Right, OK, what?"

"Right, OK, what're you waiting for?"

Pike shrugged. "Well … a bush?"

"By the Goddess Aquasis Marinas, you're a funny one. Use the seat." He slammed the shutter closed.

Pike strolled around the room, scratching his head and causing a shower of dandruff. He re-examined the seat, wondering what the guard could have meant.

"Hmmm, use the seat …"

He wandered around some more, now feeling very uncomfortable.

"Oh!" he snapped, smacking his forehead with his right hand. "The seat! Yes, of course, the seat!"

*

Sometime later, Pike was escorted to a windowless room that lay deep within the palace. It was very ornate, with wood panelling and lots of bench seats. At the far end of it was a raised dais on which was mounted a wood-panelled enclosure. On either side of it, on the back wall, was a large door. Pike was led to a bench directly in front of the enclosure and was told to sit. He did so and yawned widely, causing his eyes to water. He rubbed them dry.

There were three other people in this room: two guards, and a man who went up to the wooden enclosure and sat himself inside it. He then picked up some papers and shuffled them around. Pike guessed that the panelling hid a table of some kind.

There were three loud bangs on one of the doors. The one to the right of the dais swung open away from the room. A loud voice announced: "All rise for the great, merciful, Lord du Well."

The man in the enclosure rose, the guards were already on their feet. One of them jabbed Pike in the back and he, too, stood.

Du Well walked in as if he owned the place, which, Pike thought, he probably did. He sat next to the other man, who also sat down.

"I declare thith thethion in progreths," he lisped. "You may be theated."

Pike only understood the latter half of that and sat down.

"Clerk: pleathe read the charge," continued du Well. At that point, Pike realised that this must be a court room: he was being tried as a thief. He had heard about such things, but he had thought courts were held in barns. He quickly glanced around, looking for straw and animal feed. No, this was definitely not a barn.

"Mr Pike: you are charged with the offence of poaching. The details are that on this very day, on Lord Nairey du Well's land, you did crush and attempt to devour a rabbit, the property of Lord Nairey du Well. You are to stand trial in these fair, open and transparent proceedings, which will be overseen by a great, merciful and wholly impartial judge: the Lord Nairey du Well. Do you have anything to say?"

Pike rose to his feet, feeling that it was the right thing to do.

"My name is just Pike. I'm not really a mister."

"Anything else, Pike?"

Pike thought for a moment. What hope did he stand, if the judge was the owner of the property? Still, he had to try. "I'm very sorry about your rabbit, Lord du Well, but I didn't mean to crush it. I fell onto it, you see."

"I thuppothe you didn't mean to bite itth neck, either?"

"Well, I wouldn't have bitten its neck if I hadn't accidentally landed on it, but once I found out it was dead, I thought I might as well have a go, being hungry and all."

The Lord du Well leant forward onto his arms, glaring at Pike. "Hmm.

Perhapth you might exthplain to me how it wath you fell on the furry little beatht."

Pike braced himself. He knew his answer would be ill received, and that no one would believe him, but he had to try. "I was riding a horse," he said, aware that the two guards next to him had gasped, "and it threw me off. I landed on the rabbit."

There was silence for what felt like a lifetime. Du Well's face was expressionless, whilst the clerk's harboured a look of disbelief on his. The lord sat back in his seat and thoughtfully rubbed his beard. Slowly, he spoke.

"A horthe ... A horthe, you thay?"

Pike nodded. "Yes. It was very big, and it has black and white patches. It's called Horse."

Again, silence. Then: "A thacred beatht? Ridden, by a thpotty apology for a human being thuch ath you?"

Du Well stood.

"I thaw the beatht you menthion. It wath near to where we arrethted you. I did not thee you on itth back."

"That's because I was already on the rabbit."

"I thee. Are you lying to me, boy?"

"Look, my lord, I'd have to be pretty stupid to make this up. I'm telling you what happened."

Du Well raised his eyebrows and momentarily glanced at the clerk.

"I thshall retherve judgement. Cathe adjourned."

He stood. The clerk called for all to rise, which was pointless, as he was the only one seated. Du Well fixed Pike with a suspicious stare.

"Bring Pike to my chamberths. I withsh to talk with him in private."

Lord du Well swept out of the room with a flourish.

6: THE LAST SUPPER FOR A CONDEMNED MAN?

The two guards took hold of Pike by the upper arms and led him out of the court room through the same door by which du Well had left. They walked down a long corridor that was decorated in soothing pastel shades. Pike found the experience surprisingly relaxing – compared to being quartered alive, that is.

Arriving at an ornately carved, dark wood door, the guards abruptly halted. The one on the right knocked once, very loudly, and called out. "We deliver Pike for the attention of the great and merciful Lord du Well."

"Enter," came the muffled response.

The same guard opened the door and Pike was chaperoned inside.

"Leave him with me and wait outthide. I will call you when we have finithshed."

Obediently, the guards left.

Pike was in a large room containing only two straight-backed chairs, a low table and, seated in one of the chairs, a lisping lord. A very large window overlooked the central courtyard of the palace. It looked like a nice day out there. The wall opposite the window was entirely draped with full-length, softly textured, purple curtains. Their surfaces reflected light as if they were covered in short hair, the way that Horse's hide shone in sunlight – so similar was the effect, Pike wanted to reach out and stroke them. On the table was a silver tray, bearing two cups on saucers – the latter were unknown commodities to Pike – and a spouted pot with a handle.

"Tea?" asked du Well.

"Thank you," said Pike, in case it was a compliment.

Du Well lifted the pot and poured steaming, dark golden liquid into the cups. He pushed one towards the vacant chair.

"Be theated, Pike, and drink."

Pike sat, lifting the delicate cup by a handle that was too small to slot his finger into. "Thanks," he said, sniffing the steam. "What is it?"

"Tea, of courthe. Now, tell me about thith horthe: how came you to be riding it?"

Pike sipped, scalding his lips and too afraid to say anything about it. He replaced the cup in the saucer and wondered why du Well was serving him such a hot, bitter drink. Was this a punishment, or a test of some kind?

"There's not much to tell, really," started Pike, aware that he really should not mention a talking sparrow and the conversations with Horse. "I am on a quest. I have to win the heart of a fair maiden. The horse was to help me get to the Pit of Zidor. He seemed quite happy for me to ride him, until he threw me off onto your rabbit. Sorry about that, by the way."

"Hmm, a quetht. How quaint. Who ith the fair maiden, and how could you pothibly win her heart? You hardly theem thsuited."

This caught Pike unawares. Although only a day had passed since being chosen, he at least should have been able to answer the question, but he could not. In fact he knew very little of what he was supposed to do, and on top of that it dawned on him that he had lost his tool bag, along with his two helpers.

"To be honest," said Pike, "I know very little about what I should do. Only yesterday I was looking forward to the watermelon harvest, and today I'm a prisoner. I just wish Moorlock had told me more."

Du Well's expression, already one of curiosity, now changed to wonder.

"Quentin Moorlock, the County Warlock? He thent you on thith quetht?"

Pike nodded, and at once became aware of a voice in his head. It sounded like Robyn.

You shouldn't have told him that.

"Where are you?" Pike asked out loud.

Du Well looked at him, askance, whilst Pike felt that his brain had been pecked from the inside. He guessed that must have been some kind of punishment from the sparrow.

"What do you mean?" asked the lord.

"Er, what I meant to say was 'where are you, Moorlock?' I was thinking out loud. How do you know Moorlock, anyway?"

"The county warlock? Itth my county: he ith my warlock. What on Earth would he be doing ordering you on a quetht? And where ith he? I haven't theen him for over a week."

"He said I was the one; that it is my destiny." Another mental pecking attack drilled the inside of Pike's brain. Trying to ignore it, he continued, "He sort of told me to ride the horse."

You idiot! No: don't say a word. I can hear your thoughts. What are you doing?

Trying to escape, thought Pike.

"I'd like to thee you ride that horthe," said du Well. "I have long thinthe thuspected that hortheth are not the thacred beathts of mythology and hithtory."

"Sorry, my lord, I didn't quite catch what you said."

"I thpoke clearly enough, did I not? Ith there thomething wrong with your hearing?"

Pike was reluctant to say anything to upset his host, but he didn't know what else to do. "It's the way you're speaking. All your 's' sounds come out like 'ths'."

Du Well, shifted in his seat. He looked highly displeased.

"There'th abtholutely nothing wrong with the way I thpeak. Jutht tho we are clear on thith, it hath often been thaid that I am an exthellent thpeach maker and public thpeaker."

"Sorry, Lord du Well. It must have been the accident. It must have affected my hearing."

"Fine," replied du Well, indignantly, "I thshall repeat mythelf. I thaid that I have long thinthe thuspected that hortheth were not the thacred beathts of mythology and hithtory."

It took a couple of seconds for Pike's brain to decipher the words, but he managed to understand. "Well, I still think they are, even though I've ridden one."

"Thatth becauth you are a thtupid youth from a thmall hamlet, and therefore you inthith on thummoning up the thilly, anthient thuperthitionths of yethteryear. Thutch thstupidity is endemic to thothe of lower thothial thtanding – i.e. the lower clatheths. Am I right?"

Pike didn't know if du Well was right or wrong. He hadn't understood a word of it. However, the voice in his head said, *Say yes.*

"Yes. That's right."

"Good. I withsh for you to thee thomething of very thspecthial intereth t. Let me thow you thith."

Du Well walked to one end of the curtained wall. He reached in behind the cloth and pulled on a string. The drapes drew back dramatically from the centre. Behind them hung two very large and life-like paintings in wooden frames. The pictures looked very old, their surfaces having cracked and crazed with age. The frames were carved with swirled designs, and there were traces of what appeared to be white and gold paint on them.

The picture on the right was of a woman in a long, flowing dress. The backdrop was open countryside, set against a blue sky with fluffy white clouds. There was nothing remarkable about it, except for the fact she was sitting on a horse – a white mare. It was hard to tell, because of the dress, but she appeared to be sitting on it sideways. She was on some kind of contraption that was strapped to the horse's back, and she held straps that were fastened to the horse's head and mouth. Her lips were parted in a toothy smile.

The second picture showed ten men on a variety of different coloured horses. Each man wore a black, peaked hat, red jacket and close fitting white leggings with black boots. The horses were running from left to right on a stormy day: the ones in front were leaping over a hedge. A pack of hounds ran ahead of them. Pike noticed that all the riders were on some kind of seat attached to the horses' backs, and all held straps that were attached to the horses' heads and mouths. They rode with their legs straddling the beasts, unlike the woman in the other picture.

Pike pointed at the portrait of the woman rider.

"Maybe that is supposed to be the goddess Equinnus Quadrupedius. And the men may be her minions, routing demons and driving them back to hell."

"Demonths? Demonths that look like dogths?"

Pike shrugged.

"Can you read, Pike?"

"Fairly well. Molag the Melon Mogul taught me, so I could help in his business."

"Good," said du Well. "Read them." He pointed at two small, yellow metal plates, one attached to the centre of each frame on the bottom edge. The one below the woman read *Lady Sarah on Rascal – 1846. The other read The Royal Hunt, Windsor, 1952.*

"I don't understand," said Pike.

"It meanths, dear Pike, that hortheth are not 'of the godths'. It meanths that before the coming of the New Dawn, maybe many thenturieth before, man wath in control of the animalths. It meanths that we can be again, and that you are my inthtrument in regaining that control. I mutht thee you ride that horthe."

This time, the mental pecking in Pike's head caused him to call out in pain. Clutching his head he fell against the wall, directly between the two paintings.

Pike! What do you think you are doing? Moorlock's been keeping him in the dark for years, and you go and tell him all about it.

"Are you all right?" asked du Well, with genuine concern.

Pike couldn't answer. From the intensity of the pain, he sensed the little bird was close by. He looked over to the window, and there on the outer sill, sat Robyn, her wings placed firmly on her hips – or at least where her hips would have been had she been human. If she had started clicking her heels impatiently, Pike would have thought her to be an ornithological version of Gran on a bad day.

"I'm OK," managed Pike, standing himself up again. "My head injury must have been worse than I thought. Plus I'm very, very hungry."

You're hungry? yapped the inside of his head. *Stop wasting time. You need to get out of there and back to the quest.*

Pike tried to ignore the bird's yammering and continued: "I could do with some real food. Then we can talk about riding horses, and where I'm going to find one." As he finished, he stared at Robyn and thought as forcefully as he could: *Get Horse and bring him here. Now. I'll be trapped forever if he doesn't come.*

Robyn blew the mental equivalent of a loud raspberry and flew away, grumbling.

Du Well assisted Pike back to the chair and told him to sit down. He walked over to the door, opened it, and spoke quietly to the guards. All Pike could hear was a few whispers and the sound of one of the guards scuttling off along the corridor.

It was as he sat there that he realised just how tired he was. His head began to loll uncontrollably. In a half-sleep he heard himself begin to snore. He wanted to apologise, but the only function his lips would permit was to allow drool to roll down his chin. He was on the last, razor-sharp edge of deep sleep when the door of the room burst open and a woman wheeled in a food trolley. He could have ignored it, but the smell was too good, and the grumbling of his stomach overruled his sleepiness.

"Ta-dah!" pronounced du Well, whom Pike noticed was seated again. "A meal fit for my animal mathster."

Pike knew that wasn't what he wanted to hear, but the food seemed like a good idea.

"It smells great. What is it?"

The woman, a grey-haired, kindly-looking type of indeterminate age, replied, "Squashed Rabbit – a la Supreme."

7: AN ESCAPE PLAN

Pike awoke to loud banging noises. He sat upright immediately, the heavy and luxurious bed clothes sliding down to his waist, revealing his puny, white chest. He knew something was very wrong. He was the prisoner of Lord du Well: there was no way he should have been under heavy and luxurious bed clothes. For that matter, there was no way he should have been in a huge, soft bed, in a huge, airy room that had two wide windows covered with very shiny curtains. Nor should he have been in a room that had decorative walls, with cream base colour and red squares enclosing various scenes of feasting, dancing and other things he didn't fully understand, but which made him blush anyway (they involved kissing, and such stuff).

And then there was that infernal banging: that wasn't right, either. His prison cell had been far quieter and not this well appointed.

"Mr Pike, sir," came a man's voice from beyond the door – the very highly polished one, all the way over there; the one with the inlaid picture of a stag, standing proudly and staring at him. He couldn't recall having seen that in his cell.

"Mr Pike, Mr Pike: time to get ready, sir."

Sir? What sort of dream was this?

The banging started again. This time Pike saw that the door was rattling in time with the rhythmic pounding. Gradually it dawned on him that the owner of the voice must be knocking on the door.

"Mr Pike," persisted the voice. "Are you all right, sir?"

Pike said, "Not sure, just now."

"May I come in, sir?"

"Might as well. You have the key, I don't."

"Actually, sir, you have the key, not me."

He looked around. There was a dressing table opposite the foot of the bed. The distance between the two items exceeded the width of the road in Ooze two fold. On it was a small silver platter. Pike got out of bed and wandered over, hoping he wouldn't get lost on the way. He picked up a key that lay on the platter and hiked off towards the door. He unlocked and opened it just as the man was about to bang again; his clenched knuckles, already travelling at knock velocity, caught Pike square on the jaw.

"Oh! Sorry, sir," said the visitor.

"It's OK," gasped Pike, getting up from the carpeted floor.

"Lord du Well invites you to his breakfast table. He would like to see you immediately, but I suggest that you dress first. I don't think the lord would appreciate sir being nude."

Pike looked down at his nakedness, realising he didn't know where his clothes were. His brief journey across the room had revealed no sign of them. He ran back to the bed and dragged off the top cover. It bore an elaborately woven design in autumnal colours, but he felt this wasn't the time to admire its artistry. Instead, he wrapped it around his lower half and tried to look casual.

"If I might be permitted, sir, I shall assist you in your robing."

"Oh no! I'm not robbing anyone. I'm in enough trouble as it is, what with the crushed rabbit, and stuff."

"Robing, sir. As in, getting dressed? There are clothes for you in the wardrobe."

The man's name was Pincott. Pike recognised him as one of the four dapper fellows who had attended to du Well the day before when he had arrived as sheep leader. Pincott was again dressed in the immaculate black jacket and leggings. The silver buckles on his shoes were particularly impressive. Pike wondered if they were some kind of secret weapon.

Dressed in a yellow tunic – a long-sleeved, one-piece affair, laced at the neck and belted with black leather at the waist – and close-fitting black leggings, Pike headed towards the bedroom door once more. He felt more comfortable than ever before, despite the fact he was now also wearing something Pincott had called underwear.

"Sir, before you head down to breakfast, perhaps you would like to try on some footwear. I'm afraid the things you were wearing on your arrival disintegrated when they were removed last night."

Pike looked down at his feet as if discovering them for the first time. He wondered how they had got so clean; they were several shades more skin-coloured than was normal for them. For that matter, he wondered how the rest of him got so clean, and how he had become naked in the first place. He pondered this while Pincott assisted him to put on a pair of socks (another first for Pike) and measured him up for footwear.

Dressed in yellow tunic, black leggings and knee-length black boots, Pike strutted, rather stiffly, down to breakfast. He wondered if his ankles would last even a few minutes, encased in leather. The journey seemed overly long for a simple meal. The corridors were all much alike – wooden panels, paintings on the walls, deep carpet on the floors. He was glad that Pincott led the way, otherwise he would have got lost. The stairs were wide and sweeping, curving down to a grand hall that accommodated a massively long wooden table. Pike was amazed that anyone had spent the time building such a place and fitting it with so many things.

At one end of the table sat du Well. He was surrounded by bowls of fresh fruit and platters of cold meat. He drank from a silver goblet. Although there was space for at least twenty, there was only one other chair; it was close to the end of the table, and therefore close to du Well. Pike sat himself down on it, saying nothing.

"Ah! Young Pike. Good morning."

Coming from du Well, the word young seemed odd. Despite his beard, he looked only slightly older than Pike.

"Hello," replied Pike.

"Help yourthelf to food, there'th plenty of it. Don't want you going hungry on today of all dayth, do we?"

Pike grabbed an apple and bit into it. It was very juicy. He grabbed a piece of some kind of meat and bit into that as well: a bit dry, but still good. Only then did it occur to him what du Well had said.

"Erm, what's so special about today? And why am I being treated like this?"

Du Well's expression was one of genuine concern. "I'm tho thorry. Ith there a problem with my thstaff? Did Pincott upthet you? Did the hand maidenths embarrath you when they cleaned you up and put you to bed yethterday afternoon? I can have them flogged, you know, all of them. Very theverely."

"No. No. Pincott was great. Did you say hand maidens put me to bed? I was naked this morning. That means they …"

"PINCOTT! Exthplain to the good Pike what took plathe."

Pincott stepped forward from the shadows.

"Mr Pike, sir. After you dined yesterday afternoon you passed out through tiredness. Despite your obvious felony, the ever gracious, merciful and lenient Lord du Well ordered that you be treated as a valued guest and that your rotting clothes be trimmed carefully from your somewhat rancid carcass and incinerated. He further ordered that you be bathed in the finest oils and then put to bed. You slept until this morning when I awoke you."

"And that was done by … hand maidens?" asked Pike, the colour having drained from his face.

"But of course, sir. This is hardly man's work. And, if I may be permitted to comment, sir: the flaky skin condition with which you arrived is much improved as a result of the maidens' treatment of you."

Pike reached up to his chin and stroked it. It certainly felt smoother, and there was no sign of a snow flurry on the table. He was midway between severe humiliation and elation. Hand maidens had seen his naked body: had undressed him and cleaned him. Urgghhhh! But on the other hand, smooth, soft skin had always evaded him.

"The head maiden suggests, sir, that you consult with her before you leave here, in order that she might advise you on a skincare regime. The Lord du Well himself is partial to, and has greatly benefited from, her invaluable advice."

"Indeed, Pincott," gushed du Well. "Would you care to gueth my age, Pike?"

He didn't care to, but felt he should join in. "Maybe a year older than me? Or two?"

Du Well chuckled. "Thurely my beard giveths away the fact I am older than that? Thirty-two yearths old, in fact. Thatth me. I look thooooo much younger due to Lily'ths advithe."

Pike was actually impressed and said so. "I'm impressed," he said. "Twice my age, but looking so young. Now, why aren't you treating me like a prisoner?"

"Becauth you, my friend, are a gift from the godths. You are to be my thalvation."

"I'm no one's thal—salvation, and I'm certainly not a gift from the gods – that's the horses."

Du Well ripped a chunk from a pear he had been holding and placed the rest of it onto his plate.

"Pike: I am the lord, and I thay that you are both thethse thingths. Why elthe would a horthe, the very thame horthe you menthioned yethterday, come knocking at the gateths of Fort du Well thith very morning."

"Coincidence?"

Pincott spoke, this time. "I am sure that sir would not be so disparaging were he to know the full facts, my lord. May I enlighten him?"

Du Well grinned and nodded.

"At first light this morning, the gate guards reported that a piebald stallion approached the Fort du Well and performed what many of the men described as something akin to a fertility-fayre jig over an area measuring approximately one fifth of an acre, before beating its hooves on the gate as if demanding entry. When the sun had fully risen, and the guards were able to see the resulting hoof prints, they observed that the horse had written a message: Take me to your leader, and spare Pike from his punishment."

It was Pike's turn to grin.

"The horse, sir, was taken in and stabled alongside the sheep. He seemed discontent with his lot and somehow turned the sheep out into the courtyard. He rounded-up about two hundred of them into another message: *Take me to Pike. Free the sheap.* He misspelled 'sheep', but he did manage to dot the *i* in Pike."

"That is pretty impressive," said Pike, snaffling another piece of meat from a platter. "I suppose, then, you should take me to him."

The boots seemed more comfortable on the walk from the table to the stable. The leather was really quite supple, and Pike could feel it moulding to the shape of his feet and legs.

Horse was waiting in the courtyard, all flared nostrils and bad attitude. Robyn was perched between his ears: it was impossible to read her mood, on account of sparrows not being renowned for their facial expressions. Pike hurried his pace, reaching Horse and patting the animal's neck in friendly fashion.

"Hello, Horse. Good to see you again."

Horse reacted by swinging his head swiftly to knock Pike off his feet. It was such a violent move that Robyn had to take flight. She settled on Pike's shoulder, once he managed to stand up with help from Pincott.

"Horse is not best pleased with you," said the bird.

"I can see that. He just got my new clothes dirty."

Both Pincott and du Well looked at him suspiciously. Pike realised it must have looked like he was talking to himself. Master and servant whispered to each other. Du Well shook his head slowly, a look of doubt on his face.

Pincott said, "There appears to be a sparrow on your shoulder, sir. Lord du Well was wondering why."

"The bird comes with the horse, like a team. They seem to be inseparable. I don't know why."

"Strange. No one mentioned such a bird."

"She – it – hides in the horse's mane. I'll show you."

Pike cautiously stood close to Horse and thought to Robyn: *Get in there now, before they suspect something.*

Reluctantly, Robyn hopped over to Horse's mane and hid herself as best she could.

"I can thstill thee the birdie," huffed du Well.

Pike shrugged. "With respect, Lord du Well, it's only a sparrow. What did you expect?"

"Perhaps the Lord du Well was expecting more from a bird that rides on horseback with a 'gift from the gods'," replied Pincott, with a hint of sarcasm.

"Oh no, it rides with me. It's just a dumb bird."

"You'll pay for that," said Robyn.

Already have, thought Pike, intending Robyn to listen in.

"And you ride the beatht without a thaddle?"

"A thaddle?" repeated Pike.

"Yeth. A thaddle. Like the oneths in the pictureths."

Pike looked to Pincott for help.

"You might recall, sir, that in the paintings shown to you by the Lord du Well, the riders were seated on leather attachments called saddles. You appear not to have such a device."

"Well, no, I don't. Why is it called a saddle?"

"Because, sir, that is what it is called in the ancient writings. Lord du Well, in anticipation of finding a rider, has made a study of these matters and has had his leathersmith make a number of saddles in several sizes. He has also had reins made to a specification dating back to what was known as the twenty-first century – some considerable time before the New Dawn."

"Reins? New Dawn? I've no idea what you're talking about."

Du Well whispered to Pincott, who in turn addressed Pike: "Reins are those straps which you would also have seen in the paintings. They allow the rider to control the horse, apparently by tugging left or right, or back on them to halt. I think the New Dawn needs a little more explanation than I can give here. What I can do is advise you that the Lord du Well is prepared to sponsor the remainder of your journey to the Pit of Zidor in exchange for you training some of his men to capture and ride horses."

Pike looked at Robyn, who was still partially submerged in Horse's main. She shrugged at him. Horse, on the other hand, glared at Pike.

"Enslavement of my kind is no part of our deal, oh fishy one. I will assist you to free Moorlock and to win the heart of the fair maiden, but no more."

Pike, knowing that he was the only person who actually understood what the horse was saying, turned to Lord du Well.

"I don't know if that is acceptable," he said. "I need time to think. Can you leave me with the beast for a while?"

Du Well nodded. "Indeed, young Pike. Thith ith a big moment – for the both of uth. Pincott: go and fetch the thaddler."

Pincott trotted off towards the stables.

"I thshall allow you thome time to conthider my offer. I could, inthstead, have you punithshed for poaching on my land, but I think it ith in both of our interethsts to work together. After all, I am mithing a warlock, and you withsh to win the heart of a fair maiden."

At that moment, Pincott returned with a man, behind whom were two sheep pulling a low, four-wheeled trolley. On it were three saddles and several sets of reins.

"What are you doing?" Pike asked.

Pincott replied, "The saddler will select the most appropriate equipment for sir to use on horseback. Once fitted, you may familiarise yourself with the correct operation of it until lunchtime. That should give you time to consider your options."

Within a few minutes, Horse was wearing a beautifully crafted leather saddle. The saddler pointed out to Pike the adjustment straps and the stirrups. He had also fitted a set of reins to Horse's head – but not without a battle and a few bruises.

When Pike was securely mounted, du Well stepped back. "I never thought I would thee thuch a day!" he gasped, clutching his hands in front of his torso.

"He's such an idiot," said Horse.

"No," said Robyn. "He's a danger."

"Make use of the courtyard, Mr Pike, sir, and I shall come back at lunchtime, so that you might make your decision known to the Lord du Well."

Pincott bowed, and gestured for du Well to lead the way back to the palace.

Pike, Horse and Robyn stared after them, waiting until they had entered the building before saying anything.

"What did he mean, he'd sponsor the journey to the Pit of Zidor?" asked Pike.

Robyn, who was now on his shoulder, replied, "Doubtless he will give you sufficient supplies, food, water, clothing et cetera, and maybe even some of his men. The gods know you'll need all the help you can get to cross the Stinking Peat Bogs of Lanklandishire."

"That's fine," said Horse. "In return you just have to enslave my brothers and sisters – maybe even my parents! A small price to pay to free a scruffy wizard and to indulge yourself in a mating ritual. You should get yourself a girlfriend closer to home."

"Look, I didn't choose any of this," snapped Pike. "It chose me. Give me the watermelon harvest, any day."

"He's right, Horse. None of this is his fault. And there are a few things I haven't told you about the fair maiden. It's not a simple case of wooing a damsel in distress and falling in love."

"So what is it, then?" demanded Horse.

"If – and I mean if – we get to the Pit of Zidor alive, I will explain. But until then, it's best you don't know."

"Well, that's all right then," said Pike. "I certainly feel a whole lot better than I did before, armed with all that really helpful information."

"Me too," said Horse. "Never better."

"So what do we do then?" asked Pike.

Robyn hopped down from his shoulder and landed between Horse's ears, facing the youth. "I think you should try out this snazzy new equipment while we consider. How's the saddle, Horse?"

"Feels better than Pike's bony bum, that's for sure."

"Good. Pike, how's it feel to be in the saddle?"

Pike shuffled his rear and pushed down on the stirrups, raising himself up. "Not bad, actually. More secure. I'm not sure what to do with these reins, though."

"I shall consult my ancestors. I need a tree."

"Over there," said Robyn, pointing a wing towards the stable block.

Pike could see nothing resembling a tree, nor, it turned out, could Horse.

"Walk over there, Horse, and you'll see what I mean."

Horse did as he was told. They arrived at the wall, in which was set a number of wooden doors.

"I see no tree," said Horse.

"Think laterally," suggested Robyn.

Horse turned his head parallel to the ground. "Doesn't look any different."

"The doors are made of wood."

"Ah! Yes. That might work."

Horse clunked his head to a door and remained stationary for a few minutes.

Pike looked Robyn in the eyes. "I don't get this: what is he doing?"

"Consulting his ancestors, like he said. Tradition has it that horses can only do that by making a connection with a tree. I think I've just proven that to be a myth. Right now he's asking how you are supposed to use the reins and saddle to best effect."

"Right-ho. What do you think we should do, about du Well's offer?"

"I think you should agree to it. We can always double cross him later. If all goes well you'll be powerful enough to get away with it."

"And if it doesn't go well?"

"Then we'll all be dead, and then it won't matter so much."

8: ONWARDS, EVER ONWARDS

They left at dawn. Pike rode on horseback at the front, with the sparrow as navigator. Behind them marched sixty of Lord du Well's finest troops, all dressed in heavy armour and wearing back-packs filled to the brim with supplies of dried meat, dried fruit and grains. The men marched two abreast. Between the first thirty and the last, two sheep drawn vehicles, each pulled by a team of twenty sheep and a shepherd, bore tents, clothing, water and extra rations.

Du Well waved them off from above the gates of Fort du Well. Pincott stood by his side, the ever-faithful right-hand man. On du Well's other side, and slightly behind him so that she was less apparent, stood a rather tall, muscular woman. She was adorned with a bronze breast plate, leather skirt, knee-high boots and leather bracers, faced with steel, on her forearms. Her lush, golden hair was drawn tightly back against her scalp, making an otherwise attractive face appear harsh. Scarlet Deadnight surveyed the scene with a look of disdain.

"You are willing to trust that sad specimen of a youth?"

"Trutht, my dear Thscarlet, comthe nowhere near to what I feel for that boy."

"So that would be … disgust?"

"Abtholute and utter."

Scarlet had wanted to find out du Well's true feelings, and it had been that easy.

"He revolts you in ways that no one else does, doesn't he?" she asked, a half-smile on her lips.

"Indeed."

"Yet you still allowed him to leave here with so many of your men and all those supplies. What's the deal?"

Du Well turned to face her. "It'th not every day that we find a person capable or willing to ride a horthe, you know. I thenthe he hath a spethcial bond with the animal, and that he will be able to train my men to ride althso. I am to athitht him in hith quetht to win the heart of the fair maiden and to releathe my warlock; he will atthist me to train my army to do battle on hortheback. Then I will have him killed."

Scarlet sighed. "Honour was never your strong point, was it? So, where is this fair maiden he has to court?"

"The Pit of Zidor."

"So let me get this right: that flaky kid is going all the way to the Pit of Zidor on some hare-brained scheme to win the heart of a fair maiden?"

"Yeth!" huffed du Well, impatiently.

"And it didn't perhaps occur to you that this fair maiden might not actually be a woman?"

"Well if it'th fair, and it'th a maiden, I thintherely hope it ith a woman, becauthe it wouldn't look good being a man."

"By the power of Adriarch, Nairey! Are you completely dim?"

"Huh?"

"You do know who runs the Pit of Zidor?"

"Dan Fairmae, of courthe."

"And what's that name the people call him, behind his back?" she demanded, raising an eyebrow and shaking her head in disbelief.

"Oh. Ohhhhhh! I'm tho thstupid. He hath to romanthe a man."

"No, Nairey, not that name, the other one, where they transpose his first and last names. I don't think romance is part of the plan, somehow."

Twenty minutes later, the gates of Fort du Well again swung open. Scarlet Deadnight left on a sheep drawn buggy, packing a change of clothes, provisions for several days, a selection of deadly weapons and her own, perfectly structured body, the most lethal weapon of all.

At the head of the team, instead of a shepherd, there was a large, short-haired hound, enabling faster movement. Scarlet knew it was a risky approach: they had much land to cross, and the hound would need meat. If things got tough it would turn on the sheep. But what she needed was speed, not some exhausted idiot with a crooked stick and poor quality armour. If the worst came to the worst, she could spare one of the team, or capture an enemy or two on which to feed the animal.

They crossed the wide, grassy plain that gently sloped away from their departure point. Far ahead lay the mountains. Had Pike cared to look behind, from his high vantage point on Horse's back, he would have seen Fort du Well fading into the distance, and the moving dot that was Scarlet Deadnight, her carriage and team, keeping pace with his small army. But, having no concept of the dangers he faced – or those that lay behind – he carried on looking forward.

"I don't understand what's going on," he sighed. "It seems like weeks since we left Ooze, but it was only the day before yesterday. I'm on a quest, and I don't actually know what I'm supposed to do, a man with a funny voice has given me loads of support and stuff, and I'm riding a horse. It's all making my brain ache. On top of that, I've lost the only thing I actually could call mine: my tools."

Horse walked on casually. He seemed rather pleased with himself. Robyn was in her regular place on Pike's shoulder.

"You know what the quest is, though, so it's best you get on with it. I can fill you in with the details on a need to know basis. By the way, it looks like you've been moisturising."

Pike rubbed his chin. "Yep. The best thing du Well did for me was to let his chief handmaiden have a look at my skin. She's given me a whole heap of moisturiser to use. It's amazing: my entire face looks smoother, and my lips aren't so puffy."

"Look at me, leading an army," said Horse, totally oblivious to the conversation already taking place.

"Yeah, great," replied Pike. "Anyway, I was wondering. If my skin improves this rapidly, and we have maybe days or weeks before we get to Zidor, I might actually be in with a chance. I mean, no maiden would want me as I was, but now I'm looking quite good, aren't I?"

"Pike, oh Pike, oh Pike. I sympathise," said Robyn. "Yes, you do look better and yes, over the next few weeks you may improve some more. But we have some dreadful stuff to encounter before we get to Zidor. The Stinking Peat Bogs are not exactly going to be gentle on your skin, are they? As for the fair maiden … well, let's just say that you'd be better off honing your swordsmanship than relying on your youthful charm and borrowed cosmetics."

"Ah! She'll play hard to get, will she? No problem for the new me, I'm sure. I can feel my confidence and manliness growing by the second. All this horse riding and leading of an army. Great stuff. I know what Horse is so proud about, now."

Pike slapped Horse's behind appreciatively: all pals together. With that, Horse bolted forwards and Pike flew backwards, landing at the feet of the two soldiers leading the troop. The next half-dozen pairs carried on marching and toppled over those in front. Amidst cries of "HALT!" Pike heard Robyn calling after Horse.

He got to his feet and dusted down his clothing – the same boots and leggings as the day before, but this time with a red tunic. Horse came back, his head bowed. Robyn flew alongside, offering calm words to the beast. The pair stopped in front of Pike. Robyn landed on the ground. They stared at him.

"What?"

"I think an apology is due," said Horse.

"It's OK. Think nothing of it," replied Pike, about to remount. However, Horse sidestepped and neighed loudly, shaking Pike off.

"He means you," said Robyn.

"And what have I done? It's him who threw me off – for the umpteenth time, as well."

"So you're counting, are you?" snarled Horse.

"Well, yes. It's not nice, you know."

"Sir?"

Pike swung around to see that one of the leading soldiers was talking to him.

"What do you want?" he answered abruptly.

"Is everything all right?"

"Of course."

"It's just that you seem to be talking to yourself."

Pike glared at him.

"No, I am not. I was talking to … Yes, I was. I was just thinking out loud. I'm in charge, so it's allowed."

"Yessir!" snapped the man, immediately standing to attention and saluting. The display might have been impressive, had it not been for the wide smile he was trying to stifle.

"Very good," said Pike. "Now get the men back in order while I sort out the horse."

The soldier turned to the other men and Pike turned back to Horse. Loud laughter erupted behind him. He decided it was safest to ignore it.

"Right. What am I apologising for?"

"You slapped my bottom," said Horse. "It means you wanted to gallop. I galloped, you didn't. You have brought shame on me."

Pike took a deep breath and raised his eyebrows.

"How does smacking you equal the command to gallop? And what is gallop, anyway?"

"To gallop," said Horse in superior tones, "is to ride fast."

"And I'm supposed to know this?"

"You are my rider."

"That didn't answer my question. When did you know this?"

"Since I consulted with my ancestors about the reins. They told me how I should be ridden."

"And you didn't think to tell me?"

"You are my rider."

"I," replied Pike, trying hard to not lose his temper, "am a person who has been thrown off a horse more than he has ridden it. And I," he continued, his voice rising, "am probably the first person to have ridden a horse in hundreds of years. How the hell was I supposed to know that a slap on the behind meant gallop?"

From the ground, Robyn said, "You are indeed such a person, and that makes you very special. Just say sorry and get back on. Your army is waiting and, if I'm not mistaken, it appears to be laughing again."

Pike had been aware of the sniggers during his conversation. Probably, all they could hear was the bird singing, the horse snorting, and Pike having a one-sided chat about being a lousy rider.

"OK, I give in. Horse, I'm sorry for slapping your bum. But now it's your turn."

Horse stepped back towards him.

"Your apology is accepted. You may mount."

"Is that it? Aren't you going to apologise for throwing me off again?"

"Nope."

"Why not?"

"Because you are my rider. You lost control of me. I have nothing to apologise for."

Confused, Pike remounted and held the reins loosely. Horse remained stationary.

"Can we go now?"

"Only if you dig your heels in to my sides twice."

Pike did as he was told. Horse started walking. Unfortunately, it was in the direction from which they had come. The soldiers stared at him in disbelief.

"It's OK, fellows, just taking a look at you all," called Pike. "Straighten up there, that's a good chap. Robyn! What do I do?"

Robyn was nowhere in sight. Horse replied, "Pull the reins to your left."

He pulled the reins, and realised they were now walking headlong into the soldiers, causing them to scatter.

"I said left."

Pike pulled them the correct way, this time, and Horse doubled back to head the right way.

"Is this the way it's going to be? Despite being an intelligent, free spirited, talking horse, you'll wander into danger unless I pull the reins the right way?"

Horse snorted. "It is what my ancestors told me, though I only just came to accept it when you slapped me. My job is to carry you: yours is to control me. I shall work so hard at my side of it that I will not have time to consider yours: that is for you. In the short term I shall be patient and advise you on the commands, but don't expect my help for too long."

They were now back at the head of the troop. The men seemed to have stopped laughing since Pike and Horse had tried to trample them. Perhaps they thought it was intentional.

Robyn landed on Horse's head and faced Pike.

"All sorted out now?"

Pike nodded reluctantly.

"Good. Lead off, Pike."

Pike dug his heels in twice and Horse began to walk. About fifty paces later, Robyn said, "Very good, Pike, great horse control. Now, are you going to just leave them there, or do you think you should command your men to follow?"

Scarlet Deadnight drew to a halt when she realised that the small army had stopped. She clambered off the chariot and stood alongside the hound at the front of the team. She un-slung a metal tube that was strapped across her shoulders and looked through it. It was remarkable. Du Well told her it made things look closer and he was right. She twisted a ring at the rear eyepiece and everything snapped into sharp focus.

She saw Pike dusting himself down, and the soldiers in a muddled mess. Pike appeared to be talking to the horse and then he looked elsewhere but carried on moving his lips. She angled the viewing device to see what he was looking at. All she could see was a small, nondescript bird on the grass.

Scarlet continued spying. "Holy Hearne!" she yelped, causing the hound to growl deeply. "What is he doing?"

What he was doing was riding the piebald stallion into the line of men. She saw them scatter before he regained control and headed to the front of the troop, walking on without them.

Scarlet lowered the viewer and stroked the hound's huge, brown head. "Well, Rufus, if that's the best Moorlock could come up with, I don't think Fairmae will need any help from me."

9: A STORM BREWING

It was a two day journey to the mountains. At the end of the first day, Pike's army set up camp in the shelter of some trees. Robyn insisted that although the weather had been warm and sunny, the night was due to take a turn for the worse; they would need the line of trees as a wind break. When Pike told the soldiers they laughed at him.

"I think," said Horace, one half of the leading pair, "that you are much mistaken, sir. I am an expert and an experienced soldier and have been on many campaigns for Lord du Well. I know the weather patterns in these parts, and there will be no storm tonight."

Pike looked at Robyn, who was sitting on Horse's head.

"Tell him," she began, "to blow it out of his—"

"It's going to be bad, trust me," interrupted Pike.

Horace shuffled from side to side. The other member of the pair jabbed him in his armour-plated ribs, making a clanging noise. Horace drew himself to attention and continued: "With the greatest respect, sir, you are but sixteen years of age and have to moisturise at least four times a day: that doesn't instil much confidence."

"Well if I'm wrong about this, tomorrow morning, when you're bone dry, you can all turn around and go back to Fort du Well and leave me out here alone."

Horace thought for a few seconds then stamped his foot, saluted and said, "Sir: yessir! We shall ready ourselves for the return journey." He turned to the other soldiers. "Unpack the minimum, men, for tomorrow we march for home!"

A murmur of approval rattled through the men as they set down their backpacks and loosened their armour. Pike slumped to the ground. The vote of no confidence by the army had drained the last of his reserves; he was exhausted and wanted to sleep. The grass was soft and rich, and the thought of snoozing there and then was almost overwhelming.

"Don't worry, Pike," said Horse, strolling closer to him. "When their armour is so rusty they can't straighten up, they'll come around."

"I hope so. And I hope Robyn is right with the weather warning."

"Of course I'm right. It's a bird thing. I suggest you get yourself some of that waterproof clothing from the stores carriage, and that you dig in for the night. Things are going to get pretty wild around here."

He did as he was advised, drawing more derisive laughter from the men. He had never erected a tent before, and no one else seemed to want to help. All the men were at ease with the idea of sleeping under the stars, and seemed to wonder why Pike was trying to build a shelter. However, after a couple of hours of failed attempts, one of the shepherds volunteered to assist. His offer was accompanied by a chorus of boos and hisses from the soldiers. The tent was finally secured in an upright position as the last light faded.

The sun slid down between two of the highest peaks of the mountain range, sending an elongated V-shaped shadow across the plain. When the last diamond of light disappeared from the nadir of the V, the Earth was cocooned in a dense, black blanket. It was a darker night than Pike had ever known. He sat close to a small fire, over which Albanroot the shepherd cooked small pieces of meat on the ends of pointed sticks. He offered one to Pike.

"You risked a lot, helping me out. Why?" asked Pike, chewing on the meat.

"Because I've seen how you are with that bird and horse. You have the sight."

Pike considered this for a while, still chewing. "The sight? What, exactly, does that mean?"

"Well, not much really. Probably just superstition and all … but there are stories of a youth who will cross the plains, scale mountains, fight the evil forces, and become the greatest leader ever known. That youth will start out from humbleness and find greatness through his deeds. He will find strength in adversity and will destroy the enemy of nature. His only weapon will be the sight, and he will pitch this against an armoury of immense power, the like of which has not been seen in over five thousand years. I think that's you, and maybe you'll use a sword, as well."

"Nah, not me, I've never used a sword. I just have delusions of being able to talk with a bird and a horse. That probably makes me mental. Besides, all I'm doing is crossing the mountains to get to the Pit of Zidor, so I can win the heart of a fair maiden. I'm no saviour, just a randy kid with bad skin."

The shepherd grinned. "A fair maiden, eh? Now I know you're the one. Get some sleep, Mr Pike, you're going to need it. I'll leave you these sticks of meat – you'll need them as well." He stood and bowed slightly. "I must get back to my flock," he added, walking away.

"Wait. What about the storm? You helped with the tent, you have a right to shelter."

"I must stay with my flock during the storm, sir, but thank you."

Pike walked over to Horse, about twenty adult feet away, holding a burning stick as a torch and straining his eyes to find Robyn. Even with the aid of the flame, Horse's black and white coat had the disturbing effect of making him look semi-invisible in the darkness. The bird was again between Horse's ears, with one wing slung over her head. She seemed to be asleep.

"I want to know about this quest," he said quietly, patting Horse's neck. "I have a destiny, even Albanroot the shepherd knows that, but no one is telling me the full story. I think I have a right to know."

Horse sighed. "Likewise, I know little. Perhaps knowing too much too soon will be bad for you."

"How can that be? Knowing what I'm up against could be an advantage, surely?"

"You may think so, but if, a few days ago, I had known that this journey would involve me wearing one of Nairey du Well's '*thaddleths*', chomping on a metal bit and being ridden by a rabbit-murdering, meat-eating youth with lousy dress sense and an even lousier complexion, I don't think I'd have agreed to help."

"Sweet talk me all you want, Horse, but I still think I have a right to know. Anyway, my skin's much better now."

"OK, Pike, if I tell you what tomorrow holds, will you go through with it?"

"Try me."

"Tomorrow, you will ride me into the mountains and be devoured by a giant, sabre-toothed earthworm. There's little hope for your survival."

"A giant sabre-toothed earthworm? Hmm … is that an earthworm with giant sabre-teeth, or a giant worm with sabre-teeth?"

"They go together: giant worm, giant teeth."

Pike huffed. "You're lying. There's no such thing."

"You'd be wrong to assume that," said Robyn, coming out from under her wing with a yawn.

"Ha! I suppose they have hands, as well?"

"Not actual hands. Their cousins in the Stinking Peat Bogs, they have hands, and very short arms. No, the giant sabre-toothed variety has two pairs of legs and a midriff that drags on the ground. They're not fast, but they are silent and lethal and have the element of surprise on their side. Still, all in all, not one of evolution's finest moments."

That stopped Pike in his tracks.

"So tomorrow I die?"

Horse nodded. Robyn fell from his head and fluttered safely away.

"So what's the point of all of this? Why are you helping me on the quest? Why set up camp? Why shelter from the storm? Why not just slit my throat and get it over and done with?" He could feel himself choking up. He didn't want to cry, but he wasn't far from it. All that he had done for the last few days was a waste of time, he might just as well have stayed for the melon harvest and then accidentally have fallen upon his sharp knife, just like that kid a couple of seasons ago.

"Because," said the sparrow, jumping back onto Pike's shoulder, "to do any of that would remove the element of free will."

"Free will? I've just been told I'll die tomorrow. Where's the free will?"

"This is precisely why I will not tell you any more about the quest until you need to know about it. You'd just spend your time feeling sorry for yourself, or worrying too much when you should be sleeping."

None of this made sense to Pike, and he found their evasiveness frustrating.

"If I die, there is no quest, is there?"

"That's where you are wrong. If you die, the quest becomes someone else's to fulfil."

"Well you'd better fly away and find that person then. I'm a dead man already."

Horse wandered over and pressed his long face against Pike's. It was the first affectionate gesture the beast had shown towards him. "You're not dead yet, and you needn't be tomorrow. Death is just one possible outcome – the most likely, admittedly, but not certain. You have the ability to shape your destiny—"

"—within certain constraints, of course," interjected Robyn.

"Of course," agreed Horse. "But the point is, now you're going to fret about this all night. If Robyn told you every obstacle in your way, you'd never get up in the mornings for fear of breaking a toe nail."

The conversation might have continued, but for the loud, explosive, percussive noise that shook the ground and nearly deafened all present. Pike leapt in the air with the shock.

"What the hell was that?"

"That was thunder, over in the mountains," answered Robyn. "I did tell you this'd be spectacular, didn't I?"

"Shouldn't there have been lightning to go with it?"

"Oh, there would have been, but it'd be hidden in the mountains, where you can't see it."

The second clap was louder still, and it caused the soldiers to hiss at each other in panicked tones.

"You'd better get in the tent, Pike, and you'd better hold on to it with all your strength. Horse, you'd better shelter under the trees. I'll shelter with Pike."

Horse snorted a reply. "Trees in a thunder storm? No way. I'm in the tent with you two."

"But it's not big enough."

"It is if I'm careful, plus I'm stronger than this youth, so I'll be able to secure it better."

Pike reached out to Horse and patted his neck. "I'll gladly have you by my side, oh noble beast."

A few minutes later, the three of them were inside the tent. Horse had reversed himself in, squatted down on to his belly and taken up most of the space. Pike was forced to sit between his front legs. He left a small gap in the overlapping material that formed the entrance, but he need not have done to witness the brilliant flashes of lightning. The entire tent lit up as the light penetrated the canvas. Thunder claps vibrated the ground and half deafened Pike. The men outside shouted to each other as they hastily and belatedly tried to erect their shelters. And then there was the rain.

Rain fell from the sky like millions of buckets-full being thrown from on high. It was so torrential that water seeped into Pike's tent from the grass outside. The canvas flapped and cracked with the wind and water hammering against it. Horse turned his head upwards and bit onto the central pole that held the roof up.

There came the brightest flash imaginable, accompanied by the loudest thunder clap Pike had ever heard: it was so loud that it almost drowned out the scream. It sent a shudder down his spine.

"I should go and check what that was," he said, reaching for the flap of cloth that formed the door.

"Don't be stupid," said Robyn. "You'll drown, or be hit by lightning or something."

"You've already told me I'll die anyway, so what's the problem?"

"Free will, Pike," said Horse, still biting onto the post to keep it steady. "You don't have to die tomorrow, and you don't have to tonight."

Pike flopped back against Horse's warm neck, his heart beating heavily and his conscience churning his gut. Could he just sit there, leaving the soldiers to their fate? Or should he go out and try to help them? And what of Albanroot? He'd helped to erect the tent: should Pike at least go and help him?

"I know what you're thinking, Pike," said Robyn. "Help the men, rescue the shepherd. Well it's not for you to do that. They took their chances, they can pay the price. In the morning, whatever men are left will follow you and listen to you without question. They'll know they can trust your judgement. And the shepherd? Well, you couldn't separate him from his sheep whatever happened; he would die to protect them."

Pike pressed his fingertips to his temples, the pressure gave some relief to the headache that had begun to plague him, but not much. There were several more blinding flashes, accompanied by screams from the men and followed almost immediately by thunderclaps.

"It's not their fault! They shouldn't have to pay with their lives. They didn't know I knew anything – or that I was being advised by a bird."

"Do you think that if you'd told them that," said Horse, urgently, "they'd have actually believed you?"

"Well, no, but that's not the point."

"No," snapped Robyn. "The point is, they can't know you're being advised by a bird, and you can't do anything to help them. Even in this tent, we might all die."

Pike looked down. A wave of despair washed over him. This was getting so out of hand. Everything was against him, and now – now this.

"By the gods! This is just so unfair," he moaned.

"Yep," said Horse, "life and death decisions at your age."

"I didn't mean that. It's my new trousers. They're getting soaked. They're probably ruined."

From her vantage point on higher ground, Scarlet Deadnight watched as lightning struck Camp Pike. She was too far away, and it was too dark to see specifics, but she heard the screams of the men echoing across the plain, drowned out only by the next clap of thunder.

Scarlet had wondered why the flake-faced youth had bothered to erect his tent: it was only when the shepherd lent him a hand that she decided he must know something that she didn't, and that she decided to create her own shelter. She did so using her chariot and a sheet of canvas that she carried on board as an all-purpose cover. She wedged its edges under the wheels and the coupling bar at the front. When the storm began to move in, she buried herself under the canvas, taking the massive hound with her for comfort and warmth. The dog was appreciative but smelly. It occurred to her that if she hadn't used the canvas in such a way, lightning might well have struck her chariot – or even her own breast-plate.

Through a gap in her wrappings she pointed the tubular viewing device, which she recalled du Well had called a telescopic eyeglass, towards the camp and spent a few minutes focusing it – not easy, when the only light came from the flashes of lightning. At least they were frequent. Scanning the area of the camp she was able to make out the men in panic, and Pike's tent in severe danger of blowing away. Still, as he was the only one down there who had the advantage of shelter; there must be more to him than met the eye. How come he had foreseen the storm, yet du Well's soldiers – and even she – had failed to do so? Could he be so insightful with other matters? Would he succeed, despite the odds being stacked against him?

All that she was sure of was that the idiot du Well should never have promised to help Pike in his quest. How could he have failed to spot the connection? Dan Fairmae, or as his workforce ironically and reversibly called him, Fairmae Dan – the Fair Maiden? It was pretty obvious, wasn't it? If Pike did succeed, then supplies would dry up, and all that du Well wanted to achieve would be nothing more than spit in the wind. Scarlet's own interests would be severely affected – who would keep her employed in her line of work? An assassin was pretty useless in an aimless, ambitionless and peaceful world, and there weren't too many men around who realised that history could bring great power and fortune.

10: A COMMANDING PRESENCE

He wasn't sure when sleep descended, but the fact that it did defied his own belief. What woke him was the constant drip-drip-drip of water onto his forehead from the leak directly above him. Bright light permeated the material of the tent, and he could see steam rising all about him as the early morning sun evaporated the rainwater. However, looking at the pool of water in which he and Horse were partially submerged – at least to the depth of a long big toe, Pike guessed it would be a while before the water cleared.

Pike could hear several things: Horse snoring, a breeze rustling the tent, and a number of male voices from outside. There was a tone of despondency in all of them:

"Ten of the best, frazzled."

"We wuz goin' 'ome today, according to 'Orace."

"Yeah, well, Horace is one of them wot was frazzled, so you can't do him for lying t'ya."

"My armour's going to rust something rotten."

"Better grease it then, before the mountains, and before the Stinking Peat Bogs."

"D'ya reckon we can salvage the armour from the dead'uns?"

"Nah, it's all sort of fused with gristle and bone. Too messy."

"So we're not heading back home then?"

"Nah. Looks like that boy knows something, so we'll have to follow 'im. He must be a great leader, even if he does have flaky skin."

"'Spose he must. Shame. I wuz looking forward to going back."

"How can you look forwards to go back? That don't make no sense – you'd trip over a dead 'Orace."

When Pike shifted, Horse woke up, flicking his mane to one side and causing a flutter of wings from Robyn, who had sheltered in it.

"The rain has stopped," declared Horse, sniffing the air.

"And it sounds like we lost ten men to the lightning," added Pike.

"Now the remainder will follow you without question," said Robyn stretching her wings and fluttering around the tent. She landed on Pike and crapped on his shoulder.

"Thanks very much. There's tent-full of water, a big out-doors, and you had to do it on me."

"I wouldn't want to contaminate the water, would I? Anyway, I can't go out there until we've agreed a course of action: namely, that you will go out first, order the men around, ignore their pitiful wailings about dead comrades, and show them who's boss. You have the upper hand now, Pike, and you must retain it. One sign of weakness could reverse it all."

Pike rose to his feet, in an unsteady kind of way.

"I'm not sure I can do that. They've lost friends, people they've known for years, and for me to start laying down the law so soon afterwards is just plain cruel. Besides: there are dead bodies out there, and I don't like the idea of seeing them."

Horse also stood up, lifting most of the tent with him.

"Pike, you must do as she says. You must gain and retain their respect. Be strong, and kick them when they're down. It's what I would do."

"It's all you could do, kick them," said Pike. "You don't have hands to actually punch them, or to rip their hearts out."

"Not so, wimpish boy who has not yet moisturised. I could also trample them, or rear up and whack their empty heads with my fore hooves, but that would merely be vindictive of me. The thought is not without its attractions, though."

Horrified, Pike looked around the tent, which now had at least a half-foot gap at the bottom on all sides. "Ah!" he gasped, seeing what he thought might have been lost. He walked alongside Horse and picked up a shoulder-bag from the water.

"Glad you reminded me about the moisturiser, Horse. I just hope it isn't water damaged."

"Looks fine," said Robyn, perching on Pike's wrist. "It seems to be that the container is waterproof and airtight. I don't know where du Well's handmaidens could have obtained such a thing."

The same thought had struck Pike, but he hadn't voiced it. The container was about a hand deep, two hands long one hand wide. It was semi-transparent, blue tinted, slightly flexible and had a lid that clipped on tightly and which was made of the same material. There were some raised letters on the lid: T U P P E R W A R E.

Although Pike could read, the word was unfamiliar. He sounded it out: "Too-per-warie. This could be someone's name."

"That doesn't matter right now," proclaimed Horse. "Cream up, get out there, kick those backsides, and lead those men to their almost certain deaths.

They will thank you for it in the long term."

Scarlet wished that along with the telescopic eye device, du Well had provided her with some kind of long-distance listening tool. She felt she was only benefiting from half of the story that unfolded before her.

First she saw Pike's tent rise off of the ground. She could see the horse's hooves trampling round and splashing in the surface water beneath it. Then she saw Pike appear from between the main flaps. He was holding a small box in one of his hands, whilst rubbing his chin with the other. As he tried to walk away from the tent it followed him. The horse's head then poked out from the flaps.

From somewhere to Pike's left, a shepherd, complete with his crook, ran into view. He and Pike hugged. In no time at all, boy, horse, tent and shepherd were surrounded by sheep of burden. She could see an animated expression on Pike's face, and she saw his lips move. He smiled. It was a surprisingly pleasing sight.

The shepherd stepped back and bowed.

A number of dishevelled soldiers circled around the mass of sheep; they, too, bowed towards Pike. As they did so, a bird landed on his shoulder.

"It's that damned sparrow again," snapped Scarlet, causing the hound, which she had decided she would name Rufus, to growl.

There was more activity. Pike's face bore a look of stern superiority. His lips moved and the men instantly sprang into action, lining up in ranks of ten, shuffling their feet to space themselves out evenly. Scarlet counted them: fifty. Ten must have died in the storm. The man whom Pike had hugged stood close to the ranked men and was joined by a second shepherd.

Pike stood in front of the men and addressed them. His back was to Scarlet, so she couldn't actually see his lips move. However, his torso heaved, his arms gesticulated, and some of the men visibly flinched, so he could only have been addressing them in commanding tones.

"I wish to the gods I could hear this speech, Rufus. It must be a corker, by the way the men are reacting. Maybe this Pike will be a threat to Fairmae, after all."

"Grrrrrrr, slurp," agreed Rufus, scratching behind his left ear and licking his lips. A globule of doggy spittle fell at Scarlet's feet, but she paid it no heed.

"It'd probably look more impressive, though, if that horse wasn't still wearing a tent."

If Scarlet had been able to hear Pike's speech, she would have been doubly impressed. Under threat of having his eyes pecked out at dawn (assuming he survived the foreseen attack of the giant sabre-toothed worms, that is), he had mustered up the courage to address the remaining troops in tones befitting any respectable commanding officer. The fact that Robyn pecked his ear every time he wavered did much to assist his demeanour.

"You should have listened to your leader," he barked at them, once they were in line. "If you had, then perhaps your colleagues would not now resemble … resemble …" He thought loudly to Robyn: *What do they resemble?*

Robyn thought back: *Burnt offerings with silvery metal bits sticking out of them.*

"If you had listened, they would not now resemble burnt offerings with silvery metal bits sticking out of them."

He looked around at the vaguely nodding heads of the men.

"Last night I predicted there would be one hell of a storm: you chose to ignore me. The one person – one person – who listened was a lowly shepherd. He alone helped me to erect the tent that saved me from the storm. He alone had the confidence and foresight to realise the truth of my words: he alone risked the ridicule of his fellow men to help me. ALL HAIL THE GOOD SHEPHERD, ALBANROOT!"

He yelled out the last part whilst thrusting a clenched fist into the air. He was met with a resounding refrain from the men: "ALL HAIL ALBANROOT!"

"Well done. I thought you'd messed up, there," said Robyn. "No one hails a shepherd. They beat him, jab him with sticks and yell at him to turn left or right, or to run faster, but hail him? Nah."

Continuing, Pike announced: "In the weeks to come, I shall use Albanroot as my messenger to you all. My commands shall be through him; you will treat him with courtesy and respect, and you will not jab at him with sharp sticks or other pointy things." This caused a muffled murmur to circulate the ranks. "In fact, nor shall you do these things to his fellow shepherd. Neither shall be jabbed at. I shall decorate Albanroot with the highest honour, should we survive this quest."

"Shouldn't have mentioned the possibility of not surviving," chided Horse. "Always upsets humans, that does."

Horse was right: the men looked both terrified and angry at once.

"And we will, of course, do our best to survive this quest, just make sure you pay heed to my instructions and most of us might make it. Anyone caught dying will be punished for not listening!"

"Pike, stop while you're ahead, for Hearne's sake," snapped Robyn.

"I have said enough, men. Now is the time to bury the dead and salvage whatever of their belongings you can. And not necessarily in that order. Be ready to decamp very soon. DISMISSED!"

The soldiers went about their business, apparently impressed by their leader's new-found confidence.

"Most impressive," said Horse, as Pike dragged the remaining tent-cloth from his body. "And just how are you going to pacify them when they start to die? Giant, sabre-toothed worms, remember?"

Pike patted Horse's haunch.

"I'm hardly likely to forget, am I? It's me who's supposed to die today, so they can just curse my rotting corpse if some of them die too."

The army moved out a short while later, leaving a mound of earth covering a mass burial site. The soldiers had wanted to dig individual graves but, as four of the dead had been fused together, they soon changed their minds. Albanroot had suggested that Pike speak a few words in respect of the dead. Sitting on horseback alongside the grave, he simply said this:

"May the gods see them into the afterlife, even though they died from their own ignorance."

He rode slowly away, and the troops followed in silence.

"Was that a bit harsh?" he asked.

"No," answered Robyn, from between Horse's ears. "Treat them firmly but fairly and they'll respect you. Who knows, if you survive all of this, you might make a better melon manager for Molag."

"If I do survive all of this, then apparently I'm destined for greater things than melon farming. According to Albanroot, I might be a great leader."

"And if you wish to survive, you need a crash course in swordsmanship," suggested Robyn. "When you decide the men can rest, you must command their best swordsman to train you."

"Great idea. 'Cos he won't need any rest, will he?"

"Pike, oh Pike. You will reward him by allowing him to be transported for the remainder of the afternoon upon one of the sheep-drawn buggies. That way, you get to learn, he gets in some training and then he gets some sleep. Tonight, when you're most likely to be attacked, he'll be awake enough to save you. Simple, isn't it?"

"Nice thinking, sparrow," said Horse.

They reached the foothills of the mountains by mid-afternoon. Horse and Robyn wandered away from the main group in order to discuss their plans for what Pike considered to be his very limited future. Just as he began to feel depressed at the thought of being worm-fodder, Albanroot, sweaty and a little breathless after leading his team of woolly animals, reported to him for directions.

"Identify for me the best swordsman in the outfit," said Pike, "and bring him to me. Also, I need a sword and one of those dangly things that hangs off the belt to keep it in. I believe there are spares on your buggy."

Albanroot looked puzzled for a moment. "Do you mean a scabbard, sir?"

"No, I mean the buggy. There's a whole load of spare fighting equipment on there. You must have seen it."

"Yes, sir. The dangly thing for the sword is called a scabbard."

"Yes, of course. Get me one. And it might be best if I have some armour, too."

Albanroot trotted away.

Pike looked around at the sorry band of men who had dropped to the ground in near exhaustion. He wondered how they would fare once they got into the mountains proper. This was only the second day, there had been no fighting, and yet there they were: draped over the rugged rye grass like tents without posts. He had seen string bags with more spine than some of those fellows. These were supposed to have been some of du Well's best men. The depression, which Albanroot had temporarily diverted, again began to descend.

Despite the help of Horse and Robyn, he felt so alone, so vulnerable, so out of his depth. Why, of all people, had Moorlock come to him? What right did anyone have to drag a poor innocent from his village and send him on a merry chase into the back of beyond to woo a woman he had never clapped eyes on? What if she found him ugly? What if she didn't find him ugly, but instead found him skewered on the sabre tooth of a giant, slimy worm, or drowned in the Stinking Peat Bogs of Lanklandishire? What hope of heroism and love then, eh?

Du Well was just as bad as Moorlock; he could tell they were acquainted. Du Well must have known his rabble wasn't up to the task. Yes, they'd lost a few comrades, but heck, they were supposedly the crack troops of the du Well estate: an embryonic megalomaniac's guardians of a new world order, but they were all just flopped out on the dirt.

It was whilst pondering the meaning of the term embryonic megalomaniac that Pike was shaken from his malaise by the sound of metal on metal and a gruff greeting of, "Here to teach you to fight."

"Great," said Pike, facing the owner of the voice. "Let's get to … it. Hell, how come I didn't notice you before?"

It was a very pertinent question. What stood before him was one of the largest human beings he had ever set eyes on: eight adult feet tall, apparently the same wide, and many more adult feet in circumference. The man's biceps were thicker than Pike's waistline. He wore what on any normal person would have been a lengthy beard, but it merely looked bushy on him. The man took a swig from a water flask and swallowed deeply before answering, making his Adam's apple, which was larger than a fist, bob up and down. He breathed deeply, his teeth glinting in the lowering sun.

"Keep myself to myself, I do."

"But you're twice as big as the rest of 'em."

"That I am."

And there was no further explanation.

Albanroot returned with a breastplate, chainmail, a helmet and a scabbard and sword. Pike put on the gear with some help from the shepherd, whilst the big man watched intently. It made Pike feel uneasy to have this huge monster staring at him, but he didn't want to upset the fellow just before he received his first lesson in swordsmanship. He made some small talk, just to break the tension.

"So, big man, you're the best swordsman in the company, then?"

"Yep."

"Do you have a name?"

"Yep."

"Would you tell me what that name is?"

"Yep."

Pike took a deep breath. "And your name would be … ?"

"My name. That's what it would be."

There didn't seem to be anything approaching sarcasm in his replies, but they were hardly forthcoming. Pike tried again.

"In my position as leader of this troop of misfits, I order you to tell me your name."

The man stamped to attention, shaking the ground.

"Yes, sir! My name is Elf."

Pike's laughter echoed around the foothills. "Elf? That's hardly what I would have called you."

"I was a small, sickly baby. My mum said I looked like an elf."

"Not anymore, you don't."

"No. My mum says I overcompensated." Elf grinned toothily; it was a somewhat dazzling event.

There being nothing left to say on the matter, Pike said, "Teach me to fight, Elf. I'm supposed to die later this evening, and I don't want to be sitting around on my horse worrying about it when it happens."

Scarlet Deadnight didn't know much about much, but she knew a heck of a lot about fighting and death – in the case of the latter, her specialism was how to inflict it. She sometimes felt inadequate about her situation, but the feeling always subsided when she made a kill: then she felt that no amount of knowledge could defeat her. So it was with the wisdom of a master that she observed Pike's first lesson in swordsmanship; if she had had anyone to discuss it with, she would have been rendered speechless.

Scarlet realised that she was looking at a natural. Even from her distant position and through a dirty lens, she could see that Pike's supination was superb (he was using a duelling sword rather than a broadsword, thus making supination possible). His stance was relaxed, and his footwork faultless. He was very nimble on his feet, and the speed at which he learned control of the blade was astounding. He on guarded, parried, redoubled, feinted, patinandoed, appelled and even pliéd and arabesqued like a true professional. Of course, all of these fencing terms were well outside Scarlet's vocabulary which, when it came to swordsmanship, mainly consisted of *"Ugh!", "Argh!"* and *"DIE, verminous scum!"* – and she certainly was not aware of the names of the two ballet moves he had thrown in at the end, just to show off.

She was impressed: very impressed. So very impressed was she that the idea of having to kill Pike, should he actually reach the Pit of Zidor alive, was upsetting.

Still … she'd get over it.

11: THE ATTACK OF THE GIANT SABRE-TOOTHED WORM THINGIES

Elf laid down his latest weapon, a mace, and breathed deeply. Pike wondered if he had failed to impress his huge trainer. "I know. Not very good, am I?" he said.

"No. Not very good," Elf paused to pant and catch his breath, "but very excellent. It is an honour to be your trainer. You have natural ability." He mopped his brow with a thick, hairy forearm. "I have never seen a beginner with such flair. All I can teach you is a few subtle moves, how to breathe correctly, and help you to build up your stamina: the fighting part you have already mastered."

"But that's impossible," exclaimed Pike. He was also out of breath, but his surprise at the declaration enabled him to force out the words. "Before today I've never been near a sword."

"Your expertise indicates otherwise, sir. You must be destined to be a great warrior. We should spar daily."

"We should? What about the sword fighting: shouldn't we practice that?"

Elf chuckled. "And perhaps I can teach you the terminology, young master. To spar is to practice fighting."

"Right. Yes. You're very good, Elf. I look forward to a rematch. As a reward for your hard work, you may ride on a sheep buggy for the rest of the day, to conserve your energy."

"I see. Would the continuation of that plan include fighting off scary monsters when they attack?"

"Hmm, you've seen through me, Elf. I have to admit, it would be handy to have you fighting them off."

"I hear the foothills are full of things that no man would ever wish to see."

Pike sighed. "Yes, and I hear that the rest of our journey will be even worse – if we get past this stage, of course."

"So why not just turn back, young master? Surely, no one is forcing you to do this."

Pike turned away from Elf and stared into the foothills. The air was heavy with the scent of the small white flowers that grew in abundance amidst the scrubland grass; the aroma was strong enough to mask the smell of the troops. The sun was quite low in the sky, but daylight would last longer than the day before, as they were headed into the nadir between the two highest peaks, so there was less mountain to block its light.

"Apparently I have a destiny to fulfil. It's either do this or go home and farm melons. The melons certainly look inviting, right now, and the bartering opportunities would be great indeed, but I can't help feeling that this will lead me to something better. Or to my death, of course."

"Warriors such as you must not fear death."

"I'm no warrior, Elf. I'm just a boy with a skin complaint, looking for a lady." He turned to look at his trainer. It was good to have a human being to talk to. Unlike the bird and the horse, Elf was able to use facial expressions to communicate, although his beard did get in the way a little bit. "You know, last night the thought of death did terrify me. Now it seems silly. I don't feel like I'm about to die."

"Many a wise man has spoken those words as his last." Elf grinned. He had good teeth for a soldier; most of the others seemed to have rotting stumps in varying shades of green.

"You're so supportive," chuckled Pike, feeling for the first time that things weren't so bad.

Albanroot had been observing the two from a distance. He approached them cautiously. Robyn was perched on his head.

"Mr Pike, sir. This bird of yours has taken to sitting on me. I tried to shoo it off, but it just pecked my hand and dug its claws in deeper."

Without prompting, Robyn flew over to Elf's shoulder and twittered in his ear like a good little sparrow. Elf laughed. "So cute."

"Oh yeah, she's a real bundle of joy, is Robyn."

"A robin? I thought it was a sparrow."

"Yep."

"So what do you call the horse: Cow?"

"No, just Horse. No confusion there."

On cue, Horse cantered over to join them. "Finished prancing around now, Pike?" he asked.

Pike thought his reply: *Yes, and I'm a natural swordsman, so don't count me dead yet.*

Horse bobbed his head up and down in acknowledgement. Elf turned to the beast and patted its neck. Whereas Pike had to look up to Horse's eyes, Elf had to look down. The pair stared at each other for a while, as if some deep understanding passed between them. Pike felt jealous.

"This noble beast is a fine companion for you on your journey, young master. He has the wisdom of the hills. The bird, I fear, is a little skittish and could prove aggravating."

"You're an excellent judge of character," said Pike.

Robyn screeched at this and flew around in disgust. *Wait till we're alone, Pike. I'll show you aggravating.*

Ignoring this, Pike sighed. "OK, Albanroot. Time to get the men back on their feet. We need to get deeper into the foothills before nightfall. I want them to be especially vigilant. Apparently, some very fast and hungry worms operate in these parts, and they have big teeth."

"Very well, sir. Shall I take the weapon and armour back to the buggy?"

"No, I think I'd better keep hold of it all for now. I might need some additional stuff, if we get through the night."

It took a while for the army to get back on its feet, and for Pike to master mounting his steed whilst wearing armour and mail. It was hard enough getting his leg up to a stirrup without wearing the body armour; now the additional inflexibility it afforded made it very dodgy.

"Got to do it slowly," grumbled Horse, as if to himself.

"I can't do it slowly. If I do it too slowly I can't oik myself up. If I do it too fast I just go straight up, fall backwards and still fail."

Elf, whom Pike had sent to the sheep-drawn buggy, reappeared.

"Master, I hate to say this, but it is late afternoon and the sun is low. We can only have around two hours before darkness falls. If we don't leave right now we may as well not bother."

Pike unhooked his foot from the stirrup and faced Elf.

"I am in command, and we will leave when I say we leave, OK?"

"Yes, sir."

"And I will say we will leave just as soon as I figure out how to get onto this horse."

Elf stepped forwards. "Allow me," he said, picking up Pike at the waist and depositing him into the saddle. "In addition to swordsmanship, we shall examine the mounting and dismounting techniques employed by 19th century cavalry officers."

"Thank you," huffed Pike, "I have no idea what that means."

Elf patted Pike's shoulder.

"Before leaving Fort du Well, the Lord gave me a book with some pictures inside. He told me it is very, very old. I can read some of the words, and the pictures are very colourful. The book comes from some time many hundreds or even thousands of years ago, and it tells of how armies fought on horseback, and some of the techniques they used. I think it will be useful."

"Whatever you say. Right. Now, we shall leave this place and go to some other place, where the giant worms with big teeth are looking for me. It is my destiny."

*

They left the foothills, going higher. Although gaining altitude, Pike and his army were nowhere near the mountain peaks. Pike looked up at the nearest one.

"Do we have to go all the way up to the top to get through these mountains?"

Robyn, comfortably perched on Pike's left shoulder, replied, "No. The trail bends a little here and there, but at least we don't have to climb those things."

"Good, 'cos these foothills seem to be turning into ankle hills. Maybe there'll be shin hills ... then some knees."

"The hills will level out soon. Then we pass between the two highest peaks. We'll have to set up camp soo—"

Robyn couldn't finish due to the sudden appearance of a huge, slime covered worm. Without sound or warning it rose out of the soil to the side of the trail and was instantly upon them, its mouth opened wide, its lips drawn tightly back, and its long sabre teeth flashing in the low sunlight.

Horse reared up in panic, forcing Pike to draw back the reigns tightly. The men screeched in surprise, as the worm drew its head back in an obvious attack position. Drawing his sword from his scabbard with one hand and whipping the reigns with the other, Pike screamed, "CHARGE!"

Horse lunged forwards. Pike windmilled his sword arm and moved in for the attack. Pike caught a glimpse of the creature's front pair of legs. These, more than the size of the worm, surprised him the most. They were little more than stumps, and were out of proportion to the body. With sword arm whipping around, Pike attacked, thrusting the blade towards the creature. He saw Elf running at the worm from his left, wielding a broadsword in each hand and driving them into the underside of the beast. The worm howled pitifully, its head dropping down low enough to bite into one of the three soldiers who had actually been brave enough to follow Elf. The other two men stabbed at the worm's head with swords, but with little effect.

Almost overwhelmed by the stench of decaying earth, Pike drove his own blade into the worm's flesh up to the hilt, but it did nothing to stop the ferocity of the monster's attack.

"SPEARS!" he yelled. "Use the spears. Go for the eyes." He assumed it had eyes to go for.

Pike heard the battle cry of the men behind him. Better late than never. He turned Horse around and galloped to the supply buggy manned by Albanroot.

"Broadsword, spear, anything sharp. Now."

The shepherd tossed a broadsword at Pike. He caught it in his left hand, realising just how heavy one of those things could be.

"Is that all you've got?"

Albanroot held up a hefty iron spike, one and a half times the length of Pike. Its tip was barbed. "Is this any use?"

Pike dropped the broadsword and grabbed the shaft. "It'll do for starters," he shouted, tucking it under his arm and galloping back to his prey.

The worm was wreaking havoc. Various human body parts were scattered around and it was swallowing one soldier whole. Elf was still thrusting his blades into its belly, but it seemed largely oblivious to the attack.

"Elf," Pike called, dismounting. "Leave it. Get its attention at the front end. Get its head near the ground."

Elf responded immediately, withdrawing his swords from the creature's flesh and running to the worm's front.

"Eat blade, you oversized slime ball," yelled Elf, waving his swords in the air and clanking the blades together. The two other men who had been at the head were nowhere to be seen.

The worm reacted to the noise, smashing its head to the ground, narrowly missing Elf with one of its sabre-teeth.

Pike gripped the metal spike firmly in both hands and readied himself for a charge. Robyn's voice screeched inside his brain: *Go for the hearts – just behind that huge bulbous thing, behind the head.*

Without stopping to question, Pike instinctively held the shaft at ear level and sprinted towards the worm, spike aimed as directed by Robyn. He plunged it forth in the manner of a pole-vaulter, forcing the barbed tip into the flesh of the beast. The impetus launched him upwards and onto the creature's back; he landed ankle deep in the slime that oozed from the bulbous section of the worm. Still gripping on to the weapon, he pushed it in deeper with all his weight. A jet of blood forced its way out, spurting high into the air and soaking Pike.

The worm thrashed and flailed, releasing a high-pitched squeal.

AGAIN, AGAIN! screeched Robyn's voice in Pike's head. *It has five hearts; you've stabbed one. Get another and it'll die quicker.*

Where are they?

In a line, straight down its middle. Stab behind the one you've hit.

Pike wrenched out the spike and plunged it deeply into the worm, striking bone. The creature still flailed, making his aim more difficult. Within seconds, Elf was next to him with a long wooden spear, tipped with iron. Together they jabbed at the worm's body until their weapons sank between bones and into its gooey innards, forcing more jets of blood to spurt out over them. After three successful hits, the beast's movements subsided to minor twitching. In a mixture of worm mucus and blood, some of which Pike spat out of his mouth, they slid off the creature's back and onto the ground, landing on their bottoms.

"Well! You don't see one of those every day," panted Elf, a victorious grin spreading across his face.

"No, you don't." replied Pike, still spitting. He reached under his right leg to pull something out from beneath it: a dismembered human hand. He tossed it away with a shudder, feeling the bile rise in his throat.

"You know it's more polite to shake someone's hand if it's still attached to the owner?" said Elf, broadly smiling.

"Not funny," huffed Pike.

"Yeah, 'tis. If you think about it."

"Not," he replied, but he could feel the tension melting and somehow the corners of his lips twitched.

"Think about it," urged Elf, jabbing Pike's shoulder. "Go on …"

The chuckle started in his throat, moved down through his lungs and took root throughout his entire being. Forcing its way back up, it turned into a full-blooded belly laugh.

"Why am I laughing?" he managed between fits. "It's disgusting."

Elf roared with laughter and threw a blood-soaked arm around Pike's neck. "You'll do well, for a melon farmer's apprentice."

Robyn landed next to Pike on the only patch of ground that had not been covered in blood and slime. *Enough triumphal back-slapping, Pike. Rip her open and see what makes her tick.*

What?

Rip her open, see how she works. It'll make the next kill easier.

You already know how it works. You knew about the hearts.

A lucky guess, based on my knowledge of eating many of the normal sort of earthworms. These are very different – they have teeth and bones, for starters.

Pike looked at Elf; the big man was obviously oblivious to Robyn's suggestion.

"Thanks for the help, Elf. Do you think we should—"

"—open it up, see its innards? Yes, of course. Know your enemy is a good maxim. Also, the men will probably want to dig around inside so they can bury their brethren, complete with all body parts."

12: THROUGH THE MOUNTAIN PASS

It was while the remaining troops dissected the worm that Pike realised he had not had much time to be disgusted at the activities of the last hour or so. Now he shuddered at the thought of the gore, slime and death that surrounded him. He could still taste the blood, tinny and tart, that had jettisoned over him when he and Elf had killed the beast. Still, he didn't have time to succumb to his innermost revulsion: it was nearly dark and they hadn't yet set up camp. It was time to take stock of the situation and to dig in for the night.

One of the soldiers was hanging back from the others. Pike asked: "What's wrong with you?"

"I don't like the idea of cutting up the beast, sir. I've a bit of a delicate stomach."

"Great: a squeamish soldier." Pike knew how he felt, though, so continued: "Tell you what, be useful and carry out a head count. Left me know the result."

A few minutes later, the soldier returned. "Forty-eight, sir."

"That can't be right," insisted Pike.

"I counted right, sir, honest I did."

"We must have lost more than two, though? There're loads of bits of bodies out there." Then it dawned on him. "You oaf! Go back and count only the heads that are attached to living, breathing bodies. See what difference that makes."

The man reported back shortly afterwards: "Thirty-eight, sir, including me and the big fellow who helped kill the worm."

He felt sick.

Neither Horse nor Robyn had come near him since the worm had been slain. He assumed it was because of the stench of the blood that still coated his clothing, armour and probably his breath. Nonetheless, he was annoyed that neither could bring themselves to talk to him. Instead, they hung around a little way up the trail, looking back at him from time to time. Robyn occasionally flew up into the air and completed a couple of circuits of the troops, as if keeping watch for more threats. At least that was something. Pike reached out with his mind to the two of them, but they seemed to have blocked him out. He wondered if they blamed him for the loss of the men: perhaps he could have done more to save them.

Pike sat on a boulder and looked towards the setting sun, glad he was still alive to see it, but unsure whether he would see another. Elf, who had led the dissection of the worm, approached him, drying the blood from his hairy hands and arms with a large cloth.

"It is as you suggested: five hearts behind that bulbous thing on its back. It is just like a normal worm, but much bigger and with teeth and bones. I wouldn't have believed such a thing existed." He stopped in front of Pike. "How did you know about the hearts?"

"Just a lucky guess."

"Very lucky. Not so good a guess with the eyes, though, as it doesn't have any," He slapped Pike's shoulder, playfully.

Pike wasn't feeling at all playful. "So how'd it know to attack us?"

"Good hearing, sense of smell, vibrations … who knows? The important thing is that you fought very bravely and we now know how to kill them. If any others attack us we'll know exactly what to do."

"The men fought bravely, and they're dead. At this rate I'll have no army left in around four days' time."

Elf suddenly became stern. "Don't sound so piteous; it's unbecoming for a great leader. If the remaining men hear you they'll lose confidence in your abilities. Those soldiers died doing soldier things. They died in combat. They did what they knew they should do, and they knew the risks involved. None of them were forced into du Well's service."

"You're beginning to sound just like Robyn."

"Twittery and annoying?"

"Oh, forget it, Elf, you wouldn't believe me if I explained."

Elf turned to face the lowering sun. "The men want to bury their comrades, and I told them they should do so at dawn. They have enough time to put up their tents before it's completely dark, if you wish to order it."

"I order it."

"Then it shall be so."

Elf began walking back to the men, but stopped and turned. "They respect you, the men. They saw how bravely you fought the worm and are in awe of you. Just don't let them know of your self-doubt and they shall continue to follow you to the death."

"What about you? You already know of it."

"That's true enough, but I don't intend following you to the death, because I have no intention of either you or I dying on your quest. I believe you'll succeed."

"At least that makes one of us. You just have to convince me, now."

Later, after Albanroot had again helped him to erect his tent, Pike sat alone, sipping a vile tasting liquid that the shepherd had given to him.

"It's an infusion of herbs and other natural products that will ease your aches and pains and help you to sleep," explained Albanroot.

It was strange: Pike had given no thought to any aches and pains, but as soon as the shepherd mentioned them his entire body nagged at him for relief. It was with disgust that he imbibed the foul liquid. The only good thing about it was the fact it masked the lingering taste of worm fluids.

The tent seemed hollow and empty without Horse and Robyn to share it. Still neither had gone near him, even though he had cleaned off the blood and slime earlier. He had even double moisturised in the hope of attracting their attention. Feeling abandoned, he rolled out a thick rug that the shepherd had given him, and lay down to sleep.

This can't wait. Wake up. Robyn's voice was inside Pike's head.

You don't talk to me all evening, and now you wake me at some ungodly hour? Come in and get it over with. I need to sleep. Killing giant worms and defying fate is tiring.

The tent shook and Horse's head poked through the flaps. Robyn was perched between his ears. Neither spoke.

"Well?" demanded Pike, sitting up on his bed roll. "Come to tell me of a new way to die? Obviously the giant worm wasn't good enough. What's next?"

Neither replied.

"So, what: you're just going to stare me to death? Or maybe the way fishy-faced me killed the thing wasn't heroic enough for you, and you're going to insult me some more. Should I moisturise again, first?"

Robyn tried to answer. "We just thought that …"

"You thought what?"

"That …"

Horse barged in, heading directly for Pike. Just before the tent collapsed, Pike got the distinct impression that the sacred beast was going to succeed where the worm had failed, but as the canvas fell around them, Horse pushed his head down onto Pike's shoulder in the closest thing to a hug a horse could muster.

"I'm sorry, young master," wept Horse. "I was wrong about you."

"Are you crying, Horse? Can horses do that?"

"I am," sobbed Horse, "and we can't. And I let you down."

"Yeah?"

"I was cowardly and ran away when you attacked the worm. I deserted you in battle and I am unworthy."

Fighting the tent material, Pike threw his arms around Horse's neck and hugged tightly. "You idiot, Horse. You were supposed to back off. What else could you do – glare, and hope it submitted?"

Robyn fluttered out from under the canvas. "I told him you'd understand, but he wouldn't come and talk to you."

"Gods! I thought you both hated me and wanted me dead."

"Not at all, Pike," replied Robyn. "But now your tent is destroyed. Perhaps Albanroot could help put it back up."

"Nah! I'll cuddle up to Horse and we can use the canvas for cover to keep the dew off us. It isn't going to rain, is it?"

"Not according to my senses."

"Good. How about some shut-eye, Horse? You going to keep me warm?"

Horse moved his head from Pike's shoulder and brushed his muzzle against Pike's nose. The sacred beast reassuringly blew out, vibrating his lips and making a *ppppbhhhhhsssthh* sort of noise.

"It will be an honour."

Scarlet Deadnight was shocked when she saw the tent collapse.

She was stealthily sneaking into the camp to steal a piece of giant sabre-toothed worm, in the hope that the scent of its decaying flesh would ward off any others of its kind, but she had to stop and watch when she saw Horse's apparent attack on Pike's shelter. She wondered why Pike didn't retaliate: yes, the beast was supposed to be sacred, but so was a person's privacy. She knew full well that if the animal demolished her tent, she would skin it alive and eat its liver raw while it watched and wondered where its nice warm coat had gone. It wasn't as if he wasn't capable, either, that young, scrawny, flaky-faced youth; she had seen just how bravely he had attacked the worm. OK, he had been helped by that huge soldier whom, apart from during the earlier training session, she had not seen before (which was strange, as she knew many of du Well's military types, and he was hardly low profile), but it was Pike's initiative and fast action that put paid to the slimy critter. So why was he casually lying around, letting a dumb horse knock down his tent? And why was he talking to it? And why, when Pike spoke, did it sound like the bird or the horse was replying to him, but in a series of tweets (in the case of the bird) or huffs and neighs (in the case of the horse)? And why were the three of them snuggling down together like old buddies and going to sleep?

There was something very odd going on here, and Scarlet didn't like it. The boy was proving too worthy, and he seemed to be talking with creatures. She began to suspect magick but, surely, the only wizard powerful enough to make things play out like this had been exiled by Dan Fairmae? The only other one powerful enough was Dan himself, and it was unlikely he would have set Pike out on a quest to track himself down and kill him. Unless, that is, Dan wanted to test his own powers. Ever since he had unearthed the ancient texts and machinery he had been testing his own abilities; maybe this was just another one in a long line of such tests.

She waited some considerable time before making her way to the dissected worm, taking a chunk, and then retreated the long way around, not risking entering the camp a second time. As she carefully made her way around the outer edge of the camp, she was unaware that she was under the watchful eye of the giant swordsman.

Elf's tent, no bigger than that of any normal-sized soldier, was close to the edge of the camp. It so ill-fitted him that no one knew how he managed to sleep in it: the answer was that he didn't. Sleep was not on his agenda … not until this was over, anyway. After hearing Pike's tent collapse, Elf caught sight of the woman's shadow passing nearby. Now, as she belly-crawled around the perimeter, he recognised her form.

Scarlet Deadnight, he thought. Out to protect Danny boy. She must be wondering who I am.

They buried their dead at first light with little ceremony. Pike spoke a few words of solace and was met with muted response. Then, surprising himself, he said, "They're dead: get used to it. Don't let it happen to you."

Shortly afterwards, they all made their way along the mountain trail. An air of sad apprehension hung over the soldiers; they marched without speaking, with only the clattering of their armour and the baa-ing of the sheep of burden to break the silence.

Pike, on horseback, looked over his shoulder and called to Elf, who rode aboard Albanroot's buggy, just behind. "Why are most of the soldiers carrying worm flesh on the end of their spears? In fact, why do you have a lump of it on the front of that buggy?"

"They carry it as a totem, to ward of any further attacks. I don't know if it'll work, but when in battle, do as the battlers!"

"It's just that, with more than half the men in front of me, and me being down wind an' all, the stink is terrible."

"I don't think they'd smell any better without the worm flesh, young master."

Pike belched, feeling sick. He wondered how long his breakfast would stay down. As they moved onwards and upwards, he noticed a number of earth mounds to either side of the track; several stood higher than he was on horseback and some of them were steaming.

Robyn, he thought to the bird, *what are those piles of dirt?*

The sparrow was flying above and circling the marching men.

Worm casts, she thought back.

Worm what?

"Worm poo," said Horse.

"What's it doing there? Why's there so much of it?"

Robyn landed on his shoulder. "You saw the size of the one you killed: that was a dwarf compared to some of them. Worms burrow underground; they eat the soil and plant life and pump it out the other end. What you see there is where they've gone underground and excreted their first mouthfuls. Actually, that's what some of the smell is."

"So the steaming ones are …"

"… steaming piles of poo. The steam means they're fresh, and it might mean that they sense the death of their sister and are running scared – well, burrowing scared, at least. I think we have them where we need them."

"You keep talking about the dead one as if it was a girl," said Pike, covering his mouth and nose with his hand as they passed a particularly pungent pile.

"They're all female. No, that's not strictly true, 'cos they're all male, as well. When two worms get together and make with the lovey-dovey stuff, they both get pregnant, so they are all female to some degree."

Pike scratched his head in wonderment. "Wow, two giant sabre-toothed worms mating. That must be a sight."

"Not one I'd care to see," grunted Horse.

One of the soldiers near to Pike looked at him suspiciously.

"What's your problem?" asked Pike.

"With respect, sir, you seem to spend a lot of time talking to yourself. Some of the men have been talking about it and think you may be mad."

Pike was about to answer, but Elf interjected. "What if he is mad? You've seen what he's capable of," he snarled, "so don't cross him. You wouldn't want to be the next over-sized worm the master goes after, would you?"

The soldier looked away, embarrassed and, thought Pike, a little scared.

He didn't like having this effect on anyone, especially those who may soon die because of him. He vowed that he would have a party for any survivors, just to show that he wasn't really a bad person. Maybe he'd invite them back to Ooze; he could introduce them to his family. They'd meet his mum, his uncles and brothers and the uncles he'd thought were brothers, his gran … Hmmm, on second thoughts, perhaps this wasn't such a good idea. But he could ask Lord du Well if he could throw a party at the fort. After all, they had entered into an agreement: this was a joint venture of mutual interest. Hey! Maybe he could invite the soldiers to his wedding – assuming that the fair maiden didn't run a mile when she met him.

He began to wonder what the fair maiden would look like. How did she end up in the Pit of Zidor? And, what, exactly, was the Pit of Zidor? Why wouldn't Robyn tell him more about this damned quest? Why did Moorlock the Warlock have to be so secretive and mysterious, and who was Moorlock's mortal enemy? And how did winning the heart of the fair maiden tie in to saving Moorlock? Why did Moorlock, if he were so powerful, need saving in the first place? Couldn't he just wave his powerful staff and make it all go away?

So many questions and so little information.

The marching soldiers abruptly halted at the brow of a fairly steep incline. Robyn flew ahead and thought back to Pike when she saw what was going on. *Trouble ahead. There's a slither of worms just over the hill, giant sabre-toothed ones.*

Pike grimaced. *What's the hell's a slither?*

More than two. In this case, more than twenty.

Great, so what's the good news?

That is the good news. Beyond the worms is a steep slope down to the Outer Grenstead Mud Flats, where the one-eyed winglekrats hunt in search of flesh – they're rather partial to the human variety.

Great. So they feed on human flesh?

Rarely. No one in their right mind would cross the Outer Grenstead Mud Flats, so the one-eyed winglekrats hardly ever see a human being. They consider it a delicacy.

Are we crossing them?

Not all the way, but we have to cut across part of them to get to the Stinking Peat Bogs of Lanklandishire.

Right … so what lies beyond Outer Grenstead Mud Flats – the Inner Grenstead Mud Flats?

No one really knows. No one who ever went in that direction came back to say.

"What's wrong, young master?" asked Elf.

Pike looked to his right and saw that the big man was standing alongside him.

"You appear to be in a dream world," Elf continued. "Perhaps you should investigate why we have stopped."

"I know why we've stopped. I was just trying to figure out what to do about it."

"Why have we stopped?"

"Giant worms over the brow of the hill, one-eyed winglekrats and the Outer Grenstead Mudflats at the bottom of it. Any suggestions?"

Elf looked at Pike quizzically. "How can you possibly know what's going on?"

"I'm the great leader, so trust me."

"OK, let's take a look."

The men at the head of the troop had seemingly frozen in horror. Pike looked out across the sweeping vista that lay ahead. Robyn had been quite right: twenty or more giant worms slowly slithered around on the upper part of the slope; the nearby worm casts steamed ominously. Beyond the worms the trail dipped sharply – so much so that most of it was not visible.

However, the lower part could be seen, off in the distance, where it almost petered out into a brown, mushy-looking mess.

That must be the mud flats, thought Pike.

Strangely, the mud seemed to undulate as if it were alive, particularly where the trail led into it. Parts of the trail were almost completely obscured by the mud, but he could at least see that it forked off – one branch turning at ninety degrees to the left, the other gently curving to the right. Both branches were obscured by a brownish haze that hovered in the air.

"These worms seem to be waiting for us," said Elf. "It's as if they thought they'd gang up and get us while we are tired after coming over the hill. Who'd have credited them with intelligent thought?"

"Do you think the worm cutlets will put them off?" asked Pike.

"Maybe they will, but maybe we'll just have to find out."

"Doesn't sound promising. What do you know of one-eyed winglekrats?"

"Vicious little blighters." Elf's eyes glazed over momentarily and he shuddered, as if remembering something nasty. "Like to eat their prey alive, while it's fresh. They're not very big, but they attack in vast numbers."

"Is there such a thing as a two-eyed winglekrat?"

Elf looked astonished. "A two-eyed winglekrat? Who ever heard of such a thing? That's just ridiculous. A two-eyed winglekrat? For the sake of the gods!"

"Oooo, sor-ry."

"No offence taken, young master. But a two-eyed winglekrat? Pah! No: one-eyed is the variety we have to worry about here. Mind you, I hear that the three-eyed winglekrat makes an excellent house pet and is very good with children."

"Do you think the OEWs would like a worm supper?" snorted Horse.

"I don't have a clue," replied Pike, out loud.

"Don't have a clue about what?" asked Elf.

"Whether or not the one-eyed winglekrats would like a worm supper."

"Hah! Now there's an inventive thought worthy of a great leader. I'll bet the OEWs have never tasted giant earthworm: worms live up here, OEWs live down there, so they'd never get the chance. Maybe they could acquire the taste."

"That's very perceptive of you Elf. That's exactly what I was thinking," lied Pike.

"Like hell," said Horse. "That thought never entered your head."

Yes it did, Pike thought back to the beast. *The thought left your head and then it entered mine.*

Horse snorted again. "Oh, well, now that you put it that way, I must say that I'm very impressed at your level of thinking – or mine, at least."

Robyn, who had been out of sight and very quiet for a change, landed on Pike's shoulder.

"So all you need to do," she told him, "is find a way to get past twenty-one giant worms, kill at least one of them without dying yourself, then roll the carcass down the hill to the mud flats and see if one-eyed winglekrats would prefer its meat to yours. Sounds easy enough. Oh, and you have to take pieces of it across the trail to feed to any other winglekrats that you come across."

Despite himself, Pike smiled, and thought his reply to the bird. *Let's try it.*

13: OF WINGLEKRATS AND DAISIES

Killing twenty-one giant worms might have proved onerous, but they only needed to kill three before the others gave up and slithered back underground. The men fought bravely and there were no losses, only minor injury. Pike once more found himself covered in worm gore from head to toe, but this time he was less revolted by it. After allowing the men time to rest, Pike stood to address them.

"One volunteer, please. One man, brave enough to come down that hill with me and test the one-eyed winglekrat theory."

The soldier, who earlier had backed out of dissecting the first worm, stepped forwards. "What is the one-eyed winglekrat theory, sir?"

"It goes like this: winglekrats like human flesh. Right now we are covered in worm goo and can't really smell much like humans. We're going to go down there and see what they do if we feed them some worm flesh."

The soldier looked hesitant. "What if we feed them worm flesh and they like it? We're both going to smell like worms and they'll attack us."

"A very good point," replied Pike, seeing the gaping great hole in his plan. "A great point indeed. Just think of the possibilities though: if we succeed down there, and the winglekrats don't like worm – a good possibility, considering that they live so close to each other, yet the worms aren't eaten by the winglekrats – then you'll be a hero to all your mates here and we'll all get across safely."

"You mean, death or glory?"

"Yep."

"OK. I'll do it. I've felt inadequate since the dissection."

"Great stuff. Now, I need some volunteers to chop up one of those worms and strap a large chunk to the back of Horse so we can drag it down there."

*

The soldier's name was Sid. Before going down the hill he doused himself in even more worm goo, saying, "If they like worm, they'll get me finished quickly if I smell really appetising."

As they approached the mud flats, Pike could see the undulations more clearly. Every now and then, a cone-shaped creature would leap out of the grey mass and splodge back in so rapidly it was impossible to make out any details of it.

The trail was quite narrow where it crossed the mud. Pike hoped it would be wide enough for the sheep-drawn buggies. He and Sid stood in the middle of the track facing in opposite directions across the flats, both holding a lump of worm flesh in each hand.

"What do we do now?" asked Sid.

"Wait for one to surface and feed it."

"What do they look like?"

"Oh gods! I forgot to ask."

"Could they be circular, with a giant eye, dead centre of them?" asked Sid.

Pike turned to look: Sid was staring at a disc-shaped, flat object that had surfaced and was very, very still. Its body was about three adult feet across, the same colour as the mud, and dead centre of it was a black marking in the shape of a huge human eye.

"Looks like they could be. Chuck it a piece of worm, see what it does."

Sid tossed a chunk in the direction of the winglekrat. No sooner had he launched it than the creature inverted itself into a cone and flew into the air to catch it. As soon as it had swallowed-up the flesh, if flopped back onto the mud with a squelch. A few seconds later it exploded, showering Pike and Sid with mud.

"Now that's what I call indigestion," said Sid.

"Yep. Filled with possibilities, that is. Let's try a few more."

The two set about chucking lumps of worm onto the mud. Horse watched in almost silence, mentioning his disgust to Pike only once. After a few minutes of exploding winglekrats, the creatures seemed to get the message. Hundreds of them started leaping into the air in their cone shapes, retreating rapidly across the mud.

Within minutes they were joined by Elf and several of the soldiers who had been watching from above. They carried with them chunks of worm.

"House pets, you reckon?" snapped Pike to Elf, as they watched the retreating cones. "Good with children?"

"Only the three-eyed variety. They're smaller and love to play catch. Vegetarian, as well."

"And do they live in mud?"

"Yes. The owners tend to like the mud as well."

"Great."

Once the shepherds arrived with more worm flesh and soldiers, they set out – all smothered in worm and tossing pieces out to ward off the occasional inquisitive winglekrat – across the mud flats towards what lay beyond.

Long was the journey over the misted flatlands that lay beyond the Outer Grenstead Mud Flats. It was a barren world, made bleaker by the permahaze that covered it. The sun could not shine through it, there was no view of their surrounds to impress them. All anyone could see was a distance of ten adult feet around them. It was disorientating and creepy, and Pike had never felt so depressed.

They wandered for three days, this small, rag-a-muffin band, and nearly lost sight of each other for three nights when the cloying mist seemed to thicken and close down upon them. Even Robyn and Horse sank into despair. Robyn tried, one day, to fly up above the permahaze to see what was ahead, but after a lengthy absence she returned, despondent, announcing to Pike that the world must have ended several miles ago, as she could neither see nor sense anything.

Then, on the fourth day, the haze began to thin and some bright light broke through. To the left of the trail, Pike saw a flower. It was tall, purple and ugly, but in a beautiful way. Its petals were long and thin, ending in sharp spikes. At their base, near the dark brown stamen, the petals were tinged with yellow. The flower stood at least the height of Elf.

As the un-merry band moved on, more of these flowers bloomed at the sides of the trail. Eventually there was a dense covering to either side, and the air was fresh and scented with their powerful, sweet aroma. Pike inhaled deeply, stretched, and began to luxuriate in the new-found warmth and the pleasant, peaceful atmosphere that now enveloped them. Recent events with the worms, winglekrats and the worrying mist now seemed to fade away. He was beginning to think that the worst was over.

"The worst is surely over," he announced, after calling his men to a halt.

"I doubt it," said Elf.

"It surely isn't," said Robyn. "I'm going to fly on ahead and find out how long this goes on for."

Robyn was just about to take off from between Horse's ears when Pike reached out to touch one of the flowers. As his hand got nearer to the stamen the stalk bent forwards. The flower head began to spin: sharp petals bent over midway to form a serrated inner edge to the wheel. This happen so fast that Pike barely managed to pull his hand back. As fast as it occurred, the flower returned to normal.

"By the gods," Pike yelped. "Man-eating plants."

"Where?" snapped Horse, having just fallen asleep on his feet.

"There!" said Pike, hearing a pitiful scream from up ahead, followed by the shouting of several men. Pike could see the hips and legs of a soldier lying on the trail; his upper half was missing. He kicked Horse into action – the beast responded with a huge yawn and a half-hearted trot.

"More correctly, I think," said Horse, "that was a plant, eating man."

"Don't be a smart arse." Then, drawing to a halt alongside the remains, he said, "What happened to him?"

One of the men, a short type with an oversized helmet, stretched, yawned deeply, and sat on the track. "Whoo! He just fell asleep and lost his top half."

"It was one of the flowers?"

"Dunno. I was too busy dozing at the time."

Despite the desperate situation they were in, Pike could feel waves of tiredness sweeping over him. He tried to focus on – and think to – Robyn, but then he realised she had not flown away after all: she was still seated between Horse's ears with her head tucked under a wing. He could have sworn she was snoring contentedly. He took a deep breath to try and waken himself, but the scent of the flowers only served to make him more sleepy.

A hard whack between his shoulder blades did the trick.

"MOVE. NOW!!! EVERYONE."

It was Elf.

"RUN. NOW!"

It was a slow start, but with Elf to gee them up they soon took up speed. For how long they ran, Pike could not fathom. All he could see was a blur, punctuated with the occasional pair of feet whipping up into the air: all he could feel was tired. When Horse slowed down to catch a breath, Pike became aware of thousands of the odd flowers leaning into the track, their heads spinning and their petals bent in to form lethal blades. He kicked Horse's sides with his heels.

"Gallop, you idiot. Now!"

"So much for 'sacred beast'," yawned Horse, building up speed, "now I'm an idiot: I must've turned human."

On they galloped. Pike was totally unaware of where his men might be, or if any were captured in the flower heads. He had no time to consider Albanroot and his sheep, nor Elf and his massive hairy arms: he could only think of his own safety and, by default, that of Horse and Robyn.

Then, suddenly, Horse stopped.

Pike looked from side to side: no more flowers. He breathed in deeply: no sweet scent in the air. In fact, the air was heavy with the smell of dung and decay. "Whoa! That's rank," he declared.

"Yup, that's why I stopped. I figured the flowers must be behind us now."

Pike looked down between Horse's ears. Robyn was just opening her eyes, and looked a little startled. "Wha-what happened? Was I asleep? Where's the army?"

"Good point: where is my army?"

Pike looked back and saw that Elf was walking towards them with a bundle under each arm. Considering the distance he must have covered and the speed he must have reached, he looked quite relaxed and casual. "Here is your army, young master," he said, dropping Albanroot and a sheep onto the ground.

"Really? Is this all that's left? What happened to the rest?"

"Main course for the foliage back there."

Elf sat down, pulled out a flask of water from somewhere under his animal skin jacket, and drank deeply. He offered it to Albanroot. The poor shepherd looked worse than shocked: his eyes seemed glued wide open whilst his lips were drawn back over his teeth in a petrified snarl. His expression didn't alter when he was presented with the water flask, nor did he take it from Elf's hand.

"Come on, shepherd, tip your head back, wet that mouth of yours."

Dutifully, Albanroot leant his head backwards and Elf dribbled water over the other's teeth. The shepherd gagged a little as the water hit the back of his throat. Then he spluttered and belched.

"My sheep!" he wailed.

"Here you go, Albanroot, I saved one for you." Elf grabbed the trembling ball of wool and plonked it on to Albanroot's lap. "Enjoy."

Albanroot cried gratefully, burying his face in the wool and blubbering his many thank yous.

Pike dismounted. "So we lost them all?"

"Indeed we did," agreed Elf.

"They survived the worms and winglekrats, for Hearn's sake," said Robyn, hopping onto Pike's shoulder. "Who'd have thought they'd get eaten by a bunch of over-grown daisies? It certainly puts the wild into wild flower."

Elf looked up at the sparrow. "I think, little bird, that you have an irreverent sense of humour that is not welcome, under the circumstances."

"That maybe so, Elf, but – hang on: since when could you understand me?"

"Since the day I first laid eyes on you."

Pike was amazed, but said nothing. He was too deeply aware that he had no idea what to do next to be able to formulate words.

"And you can understand Horse as well?"

"Aye, more than you'd know. He, on the other hand, already knew this, being a sacred beast, an' all."

"How?"

"Just a knack."

Words began to form in Pike's head. They worked their way down into his throat and permeated his lips. "I thought there was something strange going on when you first met Horse. You gave each other a look."

"Hmm, I thought you'd noticed, young master. It was then that I first saw your potential."

Pike leant back and gazed at the sky. It was now a steely grey colour.

"That would be my potential to lose an entire army in the space of days, would it?" His tone was steady and edged with cynicism.

"That and other stuff. It's a testament to your resilience that you are standing here whilst many others have fallen."

On hearing that, rage burned within Pike's gut.

"Ha! It's a testament to my cowardly behaviour and Horse's ability to run fast, more like." He threw his arms out in exasperation. "What resilience do I have? None, that's what."

Without warning, Pike drew his sword and lunged at Elf.

"What the—"

Pike's blade pierced a creature that had appeared as if from nowhere behind Elf, who was now prostrate on the ground. He withdrew the blade and kicked the creature over to see what it was.

"AH! Now that's the resilience I was speaking of," said Elf. "There you were, right in the middle of a doom and gloom sermon, and you still managed to spear a bad 'un. Saved my life, I suppose."

The creature was nearly as tall as Pike, covered in black hair and it bled black blood. Its face bore a pig-like snout with fangs over hanging the lower lip. It was immensely muscular, evil-looking and, thanks to Pike's fast reactions, dead.

"This must be one of the creatures from the Stinking Peat Bogs," declared Horse.

"You may be right, most honourable and sacred beast," agreed Elf.

Pike turned away from the black creature and looked around. The land was very flat and treeless. To either side of the trail it was deep green. It looked firm enough; no signs of a peat bog that he could see, but the smell in the air did indicate the possibility of a stinking one being close by. He focused his eyes further down the trail. The sky was starting to darken and it looked like bad weather might soon be upon them, but that didn't stop him from seeing something ahead.

"I think there's a sign down there," he said, pointing at a small board on a post, some two hundred adult feet away.

With Albanroot and the woolly bundle following a short distance behind them like sheep, Pike and the others set off to see what was on the sign. This time Pike walked, leading Horse to allow him some rest after the panic of earlier. Elf was just behind Horse, with Robyn occupying his left shoulder.

They stopped when the carved writing on the wooden board was legible:

Welcome to the Stinking Peat Bogs of Lanklandishire
Please purchase your protective breathing apparatus
at the toll booth situated five minutes hence. Enjoy

your journey, and stick to the path provided.

In much smaller text beneath this, it continued:

The toll collector, his staff
and his associates cannot be held responsible
for any deaths or injuries resulting from
passage along this trail.
Have a nice day.

Just below that, someone had nailed a small notice with words painted on it in neat script:

Dogwyn's Funeral Services
Everything you need to bid your loved
ones farewell.
All deities catered for. Reasonable prices.
Group bookings a speciality.
First left turn after exiting the
Stinking Peat Bogs

14: THE GREAT BOOK

Pike pointed to the first part of the sign. "What does purchase mean?" he asked.

Elf answered. "In this instance it means you give the toll collector money and he gives you stuff in return, including the right to travel on this path, it seems."

"And money is … ?"

"It's what civilised society uses in place of bartering. For example, if you have a bag of melons and I want it, then instead of giving you, say, a bag of oranges in return, I give you some money."

"And what use is that to me?" asked Pike, not convinced.

"You can use the money to buy something else."

"You could just give me the oranges: save me having to go and buy some."

"But you can choose what to buy. You could buy meat."

"Why would anyone think this is a good idea? Anyway, we don't have any of this money stuff."

Elf dug out a pouch from inside his animal skin clothing. "I have some from the du Well Estate. I hope it's legal tender here." He tipped out some small coins and counted them. "Hmm, twenty-five du Well Crowns. I hope it's enough."

"So do I. It's not as if we have any oranges to trade, is it?" Pike muttered, walking on.

The toll booth lay to the right of the path. A scruffy man with rotten teeth, straggly, greasy and thinning hair, unwashed skin and very poor taste in sack-cloth design sat on a low wooden stool in front of it. The booth was more like a substantial shed that had been painted with a black, oily substance to preserve it from the elements. As they approached, the man said, "That's a sacred beast you're leading."

Pike stopped and patted Horse on the neck. "Yes, and a fine one it is, too."

"What is that thing about its back?" asked the man.

"A saddle. It enables me to ride the sacred beast."

The man stood up slowly and stepped towards them.

"You ride the sacred beast? You actually get up on its back, and it allows you to?"

"Yep."

"By the power of Maxfumo, the Stench God of Lanklandishire!" he proclaimed, falling to his knees. "Are you the one?"

Pike looked doubtfully towards Elf, who was next to him, and then back to the grovelling figure on the ground. "Well, I'm the one who rides this horse, if that's what you mean."

"Awrgh!" yelped the man, as if in pain. "Are you the one about whom it is written: *'and he shall brave the wrath of the sacred beast, and set forth to smite the enemy of natural order. He shall journey to Zidor where he shall slay the beast'*: are you he?"

Again, Pike looked towards Elf, but the big man just shrugged.

"I can't deny I've braved more than a little of the sacred beast's wrath. I mean, when I first started to ride him he'd throw me off, and then I'd get back on, and off I'd go again. And we are headed for the Pit of Zidor, but only to win the heart of a fair maiden. I'm not out to do any smiting or anything. That's all, really."

"A fair maiden, you say?"

Pike nodded.

"Then you are surely HE, about whom it is written: *'And he shall lead the world through his compassion and knowledge of the ancient magicks, protecting all from the evils of old technology.'* You are truly the one. It is true: it has been writ."

The man rose from the ground and bowed. As he straightened up, Pike said, "All this stuff about it being written: where is it written, eh? Everyone tells me I have this great future and everything, but where the hell is it written? Tell me."

"In the Great Book, of course."

"Ah, the Great Book. And where is this Great Book?"

The man looked around at Elf, Robyn, Albanroot and his sheep. He looked back at Pike and answered, "It is in the Great Hall of Books, of course."

"And you've seen this Great Book in the Great Hall of Books yourself, have you?"

"Well … no, not exactly. I, erm—"

"So for all you know, then, this crap about my future might not actually be written down anywhere. What do you have to say about that, eh?"

The man smiled, his grey-green teeth glistening with spit. "I have a copy, right here in my hut; that is what I have to say. Shall I show you?"

Pike felt deflated.

"Don't look at it, Pike," urged Robyn. "It won't do you any good."

"I agree," whispered Elf. "To see one's own future too far in advance can lead to tragic consequences. I think the way this annoying bird and Horse have drip fed the information so far is admirable."

"Right, I'll take that into account," whispered Pike. Then, to the toll collector, he said. "Show it to me."

The toll collector led Pike, Elf and Robyn into the hut. Albanroot, the sheep and Horse stayed outside. Albanroot still seemed to be in a state of shock; he responded to instructions to walk, stop, sit, et cetera, but he lacked the ability to think for himself.

The inside of the shack was pretty much the same as the outside, though less clean. It was dingy and stank of things that Pike would rather not think about. There was a table in the centre of the floor and a pile of straw, topped with sacks, against one wall – this was probably the man's bed. A few ashes glowed in a fire grate in the middle of another wall, but there was not enough heat to send any smoke out of the stone chimney above or to take the chill away from the dank air.

There was a closed book on the table. Pike wandered over to it without prompting. It was leather bound and primitive looking. Stamped into its front cover was the title: *A Copy of the Great Book*. He opened it. Inside the front cover were the handwritten words: *'I certify that this is a faithful copy of the volume stored within the Great Hall of Books'*. It was signed by Quentin Moorlock, the County Warlock.

"How did you come by this?" asked Pike, not yet daring to turn another page.

"The County Warlock himself gave it to me. Not the Lanklandishire County Warlock, mind. This one came from another county."

"Ooze?" suggested Pike.

"Oh, sorry, I thought I'd stopped that happening," he replied, dabbing a crusted sore on his neck with a dirty rag that he produced, seemingly from nowhere. "It's the rancid air around here. Brings up the boils something rotten, it does."

"Not your festering boils, man, the County of Ooze. It's where Moorlock comes from," said Elf. "When did he give this to you?"

"Oh, well, now you're asking. Don't really know. I don't keep time round here. I get up at dawn and rest at dusk. One day slips into the next and—"

"Approximately!" snapped Elf.

"Maybe a year ago."

"A year. Are you sure?" asked Pike.

"Or six months, possibly."

"A year or six months," snarled Elf. "Thank you for your preciseness. Did he leave any kind of message that should be passed onto The One?"

The toll collector smiled and inflated his chest. "Indeed he did."

Pike, Elf and Robyn waited expectantly for him to reveal all, but the man just beamed his smile at them.

"And that message would be what?" urged Pike.

"He said you were to have free passage through the Stinking Peat Bogs and that I wasn't to show you the copy of the Great Book." The smile dropped off his face. "Oh. Oh dear!"

Elf growled and started to withdraw his sword.

"Put it away, Elf," snapped Pike. "It's too late to worry about that now."

Elf immediately obeyed, but he didn't look happy to oblige.

"Now," continued Pike, "show me where it is written."

15: THE STINKING PEAT BOGS OF LANKLANDISHIRE, AND BEYOND

"I can't believe he charged us the entire twenty-five du Well crowns," complained Elf, his voice muffled by a roll of fabric padding and a leather strap. "Free passage, that's what Moorlock told him: free passage."

"Well it would have helped if Moorlock had told him free breathing gear as well," answered Pike, similarly muffled. "Mind you, he did throw in the copy of the Great Book as a freebie. Quite decent of him, really."

Elf looked to the sky, rolling his eyeballs. "The youth of today: no appreciation of the value of money."

"Why would he appreciate it? He's never used it." interjected Horse, who was wearing an oversized feedbag stuffed with sacks over his muzzle. "Pike may have no concept of monetary value, but I'll bet he knows the exchange rate of every freshly grown product in Ooze."

"The only fresh product grown in Ooze is melon, so that wouldn't be too difficult," pointed out Robyn.

Pike tried to ignore the banter. He was on horseback once more with Elf alongside him and Robyn hopping between the big man and Horse's head. Albanroot followed on, more sheep than shepherd. Often, when Pike looked back, the poor man would be carrying the one remaining sheep, a vacant look in his eyes. Probably he was slack-jawed as well, but his eyes were the only part of his face visible. Like Pike and Elf, his mouth and nose were swathed in fabric and leather strapping; even the sheep's muzzle was protected. Only Robyn was able to breathe in the rancid fumes of the peat bog with impunity, but she didn't know why.

Even with the breathing gear, Pike found the stench of the bog almost overwhelming. His eyes stung. He was glad that he was able to moisturise his face before applying the cloth to his skin, as he feared that the improvement to his complexion might be undone if it were exposed without protection. The toll collector had given them some gauze to wrap around their eyes, should the vapours become unbearable: it was a fabric with a loose and wide weave, which would allow the wearer to still see if it were double-wrapped around. After having seen the ugly black thing that tried to attack Elf earlier, Pike was reluctant to mask his eyes until it was absolutely necessary.

"So, young master, now you possess this copy of the Great Book that may or may not map out your future, what do you intend doing with it?" asked Elf.

"I thought I might try to read it at night time, under the glow of the camp fire."

"Praise the gods for that," Elf muttered.

"What do you mean? I thought you didn't want me to read it at all."

"I don't and, indeed, it's unlikely that you will – at least until we get to the Pacific Plains."

"Eh?"

"Look around, young Pike: we're in a peat bog filled with rancid vapours and noxious gasses. Were we to actually find a piece of land dry enough to set up camp and to light a camp fire, we'd probably blow ourselves up."

"We could light a fire on the trail, that's pretty dry."

"Only in comparison to what lies to either side. And remember: gasses, explosions … nasty stuff."

"In that case," announced Pike, withdrawing the Great Book from his saddle bag, "I shall read and ride at the same time. Elf and Robyn, keep watch. Be alert to anything that might leap out and kill us."

He began to read, vaguely aware of intermittent conversation between bird and giant. He had barely got past the inscription from Moorlock when his mind veered off track. He wondered why Elf hadn't told him that he was able to understand and communicate with Robyn and Horse. Should Elf's deceit be regarded as a sign that he couldn't be trusted? Maybe, but there was something inherently trustworthy about him – not least of which was the fact they had faced giant sabre-toothed worms and one-eyed winglekrats together. Plus he had schooled Pike through swordsmanship.

"LOOK OUT!" yelled Elf.

Horse stopped suddenly. Instinctively and rapidly, Pike drew his sword – just in time to skewer a black creature that flew in his direction from over Elf's head. He tilted his sword down and the creature slid off it and onto the ground. Still holding both the Great Book and his sword, Pike jumped down from the saddle and drove his blade through the creature's windpipe, just to be sure.

"Tricky critters, these bog dwellers," proclaimed Elf. "I thought it was going for my throat, but it leapt over to have a go at you."

"Hmmm. You didn't send it my way to stop me reading the Great Book, by any chance, did you?"

"I find that comment highly offensive. If you doubt me, ask Robyn what happened."

He didn't need to. In fact, Pike regretted his words before Elf had responded.

"Sorry, Elf."

"Accepted. Let's be on our way."

This time, Pike concentrated on the book. It was immensely boring stuff to begin with. One heading was *Genealogy*. He didn't know what that meant, but it looked interesting. He checked the index and looked up his name, of which there was no mention. He looked up *The One*, and could find nothing, so finally looked up *One* on its own. He found it listed as *One, The.*

There were numerous sub-headings under *One, The*, such as *Arrival* and *The Rise* of, plus various page numbers where The One was listed, including those shown to him by the toll collector, but what caught his eye was *Genealogy*. That word again, and an entry relating to him.

"Anyone know what genealogy means?"

"Yes," answered Horse. "It is to do with one's ancestors. I could probably have traced my genealogy through many millennia to the Arabian horses of old … but we horses never learned to keep written records."

Pike flicked to the correct page. There was a brief statement declaring that this was the true line of ascent to The One. The page opposite was thicker than the others in the book; this was because it was folded over several times. He carefully unfolded it and was presented with a large sheet of paper on which were drawn numerous boxes containing writing, and these were linked by a series of lines. The bottom box contained the words *The One.* It was linked to two other boxes by a vertical line that joined onto a horizontal one. On the left side of the horizontal line was a box displaying Aradrick of Ooze; on the right was a box showing Bess of Ooze.

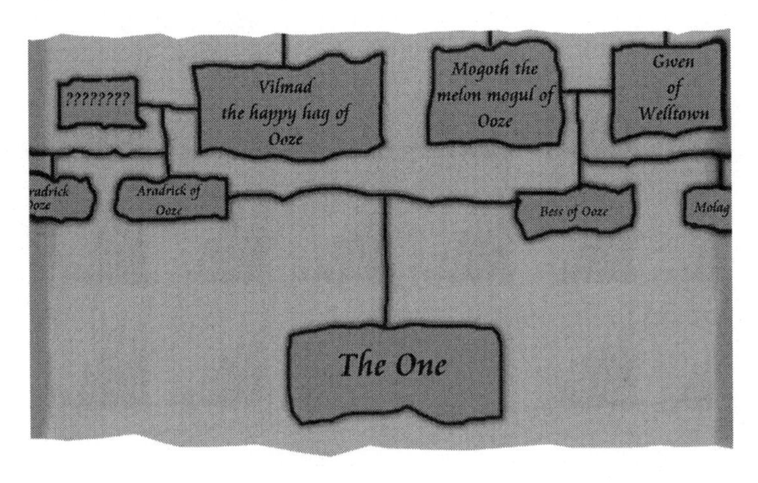

Pike showed the page to Elf as they walked on. "What is this?" he asked.

"Looks like a family tree. Normally, only the like of Lord du Well would have one drawn up, just to prove his noble blood."

"Right … Aradrick and Bess: they're my parents."

"And?"

"So what do these lines mean?"

"Right, stop the horse. This line here, linking Aradrick to Bess, indicates they were either married or they bred. The line poking out from between them leads to their off-spring. In this case, The One. You."

"No! Not necessarily me. They had many children. I had lots of brothers – though admittedly, I've since found out some were uncles – but I'm not the only one. Maybe there was a mistake."

"No way," said Robyn, preening under a wing as she stood on Elf's right shoulder. "Moorlock wouldn't have made a mistake like that. You were chosen; you are The One."

"Oh. What does this mean?" Pike pointed to the box to the right of Bess. Molag's name was in it.

"That means that Molag the Mad Melon Mogul is your mother's brother, otherwise known as your uncle," said Robyn.

"OK, that might be why Molag favours me with the melon stewardship. Strange that Mum never mentioned he was her brother."

"Not so strange," replied Horse. "He is really insane, you know. Too much time alone in the melon plantation can addle a man's brain – especially if they are taunted by, say, a wild stallion." Horse cleared his throat at this point "Who'd want to admit they were related to him?"

"Point taken. So my grannies were Vilmad and Gwen. I know Molag's mother is dead, so Gwen's out of the picture, so Gran must be Vilmad – or Vilmad the Happy Hag, as it says here. Why does the box next to hers have lots of question marks in it?"

"Hmm, delicate stuff, I fancy," said Elf, scratching his beard. "How many children did your gran have?"

Pike thought for a few seconds, trying to remember what his mother had told him. Aradrick, Baradrick, Caradrick, Daradrick, Earadrick, Faradrick …where did it stop? Ah, Naradrick and Bert. "Fifteen," he announced.

"Right, I think that proves my theory. Eight question marks indicate eight unknown (or un-named) fathers."

Pike didn't react immediately, but pondered the implications.

"Maybe they should have called her Vilmad the Happy Harlot," suggested Robyn.

"Oi, that's my gran you're talking about."

"I know. A great woman. She was going to eat me, you know."

"Human nature. She was hungry and doesn't get much meat."

"It's sparrow nature not to be eaten by old hags – or harlots, for that matter."

"And she has no respect for horses," added Horse. "A 'filthy mule', I believe she called me."

Pike sighed. "OK, she's not perfect, but who is?"

"Well, I don't like to brag," said Horse, looking back over his shoulder at Pike.

Before Horse could continue he was stopped short by Elf, clamping his sack-covered muzzle with his big hairy hands. "That's enough nonsense from the livestock. You're only sacred in the eyes of the masses, we here no longer believe it. Let us continue our journey."

And so they did.

Pike carried on flicking through the Great Book. There was a section concerning spells and hexes, aptly titled Concerning Spells and Hexes, and another called Strategies. Of The One there was little more mention. He had to put the book away when the fumes from the peat bog became too intense for him to read anymore. The group stopped and applied their eye-gauzes. Elf assisted Albanroot with his, and tied one on the sheep. Even Robyn found this part hard going. Instead of sitting in one of her usual perching spots she flew high above, avoiding the acrid aroma.

Elf seemed to cope remarkably well, given that the enormous size of his lungs must have meant he was taking in more gas than any of the others. Pike guessed that his gigantic body must have been able to deal with it more efficiently than those of a smaller scale.

After what seemed like an age, Robyn thought down to them: *There's a sign up ahead.*

She was right, but it took a very long time for the group to reach it. By the time they did, Pike had almost passed out. Elf slapped his cheeks to waken him. He had already removed his own gauze and now started on Pike's.

"This is great news, young master. Look."

The sign was similar to the one they had seen earlier.

You are now leaving the Stinking Peat Bogs of Lanklandishire. The management hopes that you enjoyed your journey. Please visit us again soon and benefit from our two-for-one offer and a 50% discount on new breathing gear when you trade in your old set. Have a nice day.

As before, a further sign was tacked on below it.

If all in your party can read this sign
you have no need of Dogwyn's Funeral Services.
But, if anyone in your party is struggling due
to a sudden case of death, please follow the
signs and take the next left turn. Call in now
for a free, 'no obligation' quote.

Prices quoted are exclusive of tax and are
valid for 28 days. The value of your funeral may go up
as well as down. Past performance is not a guarantee of future
burials. Payment plan available at 1025% APR typical. All funeral
payments will be secured against the value of
anything the paying party owns. You may lose your home, your
grave and your casket, and be disinterred if you or your surviving
relatives/friends do not keep up with the payments.

"That's a relief," sighed Pike. "The stench of this place has been indescribable."

"I wouldn't say that," said Horse, "it reminded me of your grandmother's cooking."

They moved on further until the smell had all but gone and stopped to rest in a wide, dry area. Pike and the others took the opportunity to fill their lungs with the not-so-bad air. Elf suggested setting up camp in that ideal place, as it was late in the day and it would do them all good to luxuriate in the new-found freshness.

The night passed without incident. None of them were aware that some distance down the track, back towards the Stinking Peat Bog, Scarlet Deadnight was also trying to rest; being so much closer to the stench than they were, she found it much more difficult.

Scarlet's journey had been far less hazardous than Pike's: she was, after all, aligned to dark powers and she was really quite evil in her own right. A good person could not be a cold-blooded killer. A good person would not relish the prospect of decapitation, which she did – as long as it was not she who was to be decapitated. But for all her badness, Scarlet found herself somewhat in awe of Pike's progress. Sure, he had the help of that big fellow, whoever-the-hell he was, but she had seen Pike tackle the giant sabre-toothed worms, and she had seen the way he fooled the winglekrats. She hadn't seen exactly what had occurred in the field of spinning daisies (there had been far too much blood and gore and too many spinning flower heads for that) but she knew that he had survived it, and that was no mean feat.

She wondered if, for once, she had an adversary actually worth the effort. All too often her foes were weak and stupid, but Pike – for all his defects (and especially his fish-face and scaly skin) – was showing himself to be a true warrior.

Scarlet snuggled up to the hound. It was chewing on some raw mutton and bone, the remains of the first of Scarlet's team to be slaughtered in the name of sustenance. She had lost another in amongst the flowers. She was too close to Pike's camp to light a fire so she also ate her meat raw. She savoured the salty taste of blood, but the rubbery texture of the meat gave her jaw ache.

"Bit tough, eh, Rufus?"

The hound growled.

"Don't worry, boy. When I kill Pike I will feed you his guts for dinner and his heart for a pudding."

Rufus panted in anticipation.

16: BEYOND STINKING

Elf awakened everyone at first light. Their supplies had run out and they had not eaten since before entering the Stinking Peat Bogs. Pike's tummy groaned at him, and he began to wish they had butchered the bog monster that had attacked him the day before.

"Not such a good idea, young master," advised Elf. "That beast lived, ate and drank in the murk of that bog. If that place smelled so bad, imagine what the creature would have tasted like."

Pike's tummy positively gurgled at the thought. He looked over at Horse, who was eating grass, and at Robyn, who was chewing on a worm. Then he looked at Albanroot: he was still in a state of shock and clung tightly to his sheep. Pike turned to Elf.

"I don't suppose—"

"No! It would kill the shepherd if you ate the sheep. He's too good a man to subject to that suffering."

"But he looks like he isn't aware of too much. Perhaps if he just put the thing down and it wandered off ..."

Elf spoke sternly. "That shepherd stood by you when you were shunned by the rest of your army; he even fed you from his own supplies. He's been loyal to you and you must pay him back. He needs time to recover from the shock of losing his flock. Besides, you might need his services if we ever reach Zidor. There may be lots of sheep there."

"So I am to go hungry while Robyn and Horse gorge themselves?"

"Indeed, likewise I. Or you could join them in their feast."

"I think I'll wait till later, thanks."

The small group moved onwards. Pike felt very down, right then. After all they had come through so far he thought he deserved a decent meal, and mutton would have been just the thing to sort out his hunger. Still, Elf was right about Albanroot: he had gone out on a limb that first night out of Fort du Well. It was easy to forget what had happened back then, as they had endured so much since.

The local terrain was flat and green, with just the odd tree here and there. The sun shone mutedly through a light smattering of cloud that was punctuated with tiny patches of blue. In the distance Pike could see that a brown haze hung over a barren-looking flat area. He pointed it out to Elf and the others. Albanroot did not react, but Elf said, "I don't like the look of that at all. Robyn, do you think you could take a look?"

"I could, but who put you in charge? This is Pike's mission; you're just the help."

"I agree," Elf agreed. "And I am helping by asking you to fly on ahead."

"Sounds reasonable to me," said Horse.

"Sounds reasonable to me," chipped in Albanroot, suddenly.

Pike whipped his head around to look at the shepherd. For the first time since leaving the daisy field Albanroot looked alive - just. The sheep was out of his arms and on its own feet. The shepherd still looked ashen faced, and he still had dark rings under his eyes, but he at least wore a vague smile. Pike dismounted and ran over to hug him.

"You're OK!" he panted, as surprised at his own reaction as the shepherd was.

"I will be OK. It's been a bit of a shock seeing my flock destroyed – oh, and seeing the men eaten, as well."

Pike's belly gurgled loudly.

"You seem to be overly hungry."

"A bit, but right now we need to find out what's over there."

Albanroot shrugged. "If you were to let go of me it would be easier."

Pike released him immediately. "Sorry, just a bit relieved to see you back with us, that's all."

Elf walked over and patted the shepherd on the shoulder. "Good to see you, Albanroot," he said. "Now, little bird, fly away and tell us what's ahead."

Pike sensed Robyn's unease at Elf taking charge, so said, "Great idea."

Albanroot looked from one to the other. "Am I the only one who can't talk sparrow?"

"Looks like it," said Horse.

"I don't think he can understand you," said Pike. Then, for the shepherd's benefit, he added, "I can't explain it, but me and Elf can both speak to Robyn and Horse. It's not as if we can talk to all animals, is it, Elf?"

Elf hesitated, just long enough to make Pike feel uneasy. "No, young master, only these two."

Pike heard Robyn's voice inside his head: *I don't trust him, Pike. He's hiding something.*

Don't be silly, Pike responded. *He's proved himself time and time again.*

OK, but just remember I told you so. There's something he's not telling us.

Well forget that for now. Just go and see what that brown cloud is.

Robyn was away for no more than two minutes. She returned with what Pike now recognised as her panicked expression. "What's wrong?" he asked.

"Really bad news. If you think the Stinking Peat Bogs were bad, you've not smelled anything yet."

"Eh?"

"Well I don't know what it is, but this is even worse than before. I think it may kill us all."

There was a sign at the edge of the brown cloud:

Welcome to the Reeking Peat Bogs of Lanklandishire
Abandon hope all ye who enter here.
Have a safe journey and do come again.

"That's reassuring," said Pike, removing the lid from the moisturiser container. There wasn't much left now, so he applied it sparingly.

"I would save some of that, if I were you, young master," said Elf.

"Why? If I'm going to die here I might as well have a smooth face."

"You'll not die here, if I can help it. Save some for later, when you meet the fair maiden. Look your best then."

"Ah, I get it, you're trying to stop me from losing hope."

"Partly that, but it's your head I was thinking of."

Pike huffed. "You talk in riddles half the time. Right, how do we get through this lot? The stink is awful already."

Horse grunted. "Even I, with my constitution, will find this hard."

"Me too," said Robyn.

Albanroot remained silent, having drifted back into a world of his own, but his sheep maaaa'd on his behalf.

Elf said, "Wrap your breathing gear around your face, put your heads down, pray to the gods for a miracle, and let's get the heck through it."

Thoroughly wrapped, they set forth into the cloud.

Pike decided to walk to allow Horse some rest. The ground underfoot was soft. He felt it dragging his feet down, making the muscles in his legs heavy. The air was rank with the stench of putrid flesh and vomit, perhaps with a touch of fart thrown in. Pike's eyes watered as he tried to focus on the way ahead, but there was nothing to focus on; the air was too dense.

For how long he walked he had no idea. He became aware of a hand on his shoulder, and he thought it was there at the behest of Elf, but he didn't know whose it was. He wretched, heaved and threw-up numerous times. The odour of everything foul ate its way into his throat, lungs and stomach. Pike was convinced the smell would never clear. His feet sank into the stodge that was the earth until his ankles were covered in wet, cloying dirt. He felt his knees weaken and was vaguely aware of falling. But he didn't land.

17: THAT "UGLY DUCKLING" MOMENT

Pike felt the cold trickle of water on his face. A new smell entered his nostrils: roasting meat. Surely he was in a dream. He shifted around, not opening his eyes. He could hear singing – the deep melodious voice of a man. It sounded likely to be Elf's.

The trickle stopped. It was replaced by a gush.

"What in the name of Hearne?" he shouted, leaping up in shock.

Albanroot stood before him, holding a large green conical-shaped object in his hands.

"Sorry to shock you, but lunch is nearly ready," said the shepherd.

Pike took a minute to grasp what he had said.

"Lunch?"

"Yes."

"I'm alive?" he asked, a gurgle erupting in his stomach.

"Very much so, thanks to Horse and Elf."

"And Robyn?"

Albanroot momentarily looked puzzled. "Oh! You mean the sparrow? She's fine. Bathing in a puddle, I shouldn't wonder."

The water had seeped through Pike's clothes and he felt a slight chill around the groin. He looked around, quickly taking in his surrounds. A clear bright sky, lush green meadow, a smattering of trees: it certainly was not the Reeking Peat Bogs. Elf was some distance away by a camp fire. He had set up a spit and was turning a large animal carcass in front of the flames.

"How did we get here?"

"Those two managed to carry us. Elf took you, Horse took me. The sparrow passed out and had to be carried as well."

"What's he cooking over there?"

"Mutton."

"But …"

"But nothing. I am a shepherd and a realist. To lose a flock to those vicious flowers was cruel and tragic, but we humans need to eat, and it is the natural order of things for us to eat meat. As long as the meat is treated with respect while it is alive, I see no problem with humane slaughter and a full belly."

"Great. I'm starved. Let's eat."

Elf stopped singing and turned to greet Pike when he approached with Albanroot.

"Ah, you smelled the meat. Albanroot suggested you needed to eat."

"He's right," agreed Pike, getting as close to the roasting food as possible. The heat was immense, the aroma more so. He inhaled deeply through his nose, his nostrils whistling as he did so. "That surely beats the Reeking Peat Bogs."

"I'd say so," said Elf, rotating the meat a little.

Pike glanced around. "Where are Horse and Robyn?"

"They've gone for a walk – or, at least, Horse has. That annoying sparrow is on his head. I believe Robyn doesn't trust me, and Horse is in the process of telling her what a marvellous job I did of rescuing you from the latest round of peril."

Pike turned to Elf. "I'm so stupid. Thank you."

"I was merely giving you an answer to your question, not hinting for your thanks, but I appreciate them anyway."

Albanroot dumped his conical-shaped thing on the ground, open edge downwards, and sat on the curved part. It held his weight well.

"What is that thing?" asked Pike.

"This? I'm not sure. There are plenty of them in that clump of trees over there. There's a spring as well." He smiled, "The water is sweet and cool – as you've already discovered."

Pike looked into the distance where Albanroot pointed. There was indeed a thick group of trees, some of which bore large, round fruit. The thing Albanroot was sitting on must have been one half of a shell or a pod.

"How do you know they're not poisonous?"

"Robyn assured me they are not," said Elf. "She said they were edible but bitter."

"We could eat them then?"

"Actually, I tried one: it tasted like dung, but the shells make good buckets – and seats, it seems."

Pike thought it best not to ask how Elf knew what dung tasted like. He inhaled heartily again, the smell of the food made his stomach positively roar with hunger. "Can we eat now?" he whined.

"I suppose so," said Elf, hesitantly, "though I was hoping our menagerie would have returned by now, so we could discuss the remainder of the journey as we ate."

"If you are cooking meat it's best Horse stays away a bit longer. He nearly abandoned me over a squashed rabbit."

"Very well."

They ate heartily, ripping the meat from the bones with their teeth, like a pack of wild animals. Pike was not used to eating large quantities of meat – normally he would count himself lucky to share the drum stick of a toad's hind leg with one of his brothers. The saltiness and fat from the mutton dried his mouth out. Elf passed him a water flask. Pike rinsed his mouth, relieved to rid himself of the grease.

"I'd give almost anything to be back at home, sucking on a chunk of melon, right now," said Pike. "I really have gone off the idea of this fair maiden stuff – not that I was keen in the first place. Anyway, I smell and look as though I fell into a toilet hole. Lord du Well gave me these clothes, but I think my old sack cloth was cleaner than these are now."

Elf sighed. "We don't have too far to travel now, young master. When we get to the spring, over in that clump of trees, you'll be able to do two things. First, clean up a bit, and second, you'll see our destination."

"WHAT?"

"We are nearly at the Pit of Zidor – well, compared to our starting point, at least."

"By the gods, this is great news. Soon I'll get to see her!"

"Don't count on it."

"But Zidor? Fair Maiden? My destiny?"

Elf looked away. "Of course. I was forgetting myself. Sorry."

"So how far is close?"

"You'll see when we reach the trees. Now, young master, reach out to that bird brain with your superior mind and ask them to meet us over there."

Their two companions were waiting for them in the shade. Robyn was perched in a tree, singing like any normal sparrow. Horse was on his belly, legs tucked under himself. He was still saddled and ready to leave at a moment's notice. Dappled sunshine picked out the highlights of the sacred beast's piebald colouring, and a gentle breeze ruffled his mane: a magnificent warhorse, resting between battles. The pool of water rippled slightly from the gentle flow of an underground spring, causing the surface to bounce bright reflections off the trees: magical. All in all, the scene looked like it should have been the subject of a painting on Lord du Well's wall.

Caustically, Horse said, "I trust you humans have ended your feast of flesh?"

"Aye," replied Elf, "but we saved this for later." He held up his sword on which was skewered half a cooked sheep.

"It is as well you are walking, Elf, and not riding upon me. You reek of death, and not in a good way."

"And what of Pike: does he also reek of death?"

"Less so than you – but he makes up for it in so many other ways."

"On that subject, our questing hero needs to take a bath before we continue our journey. Please excuse him and move away from the watering hole."

"First he pollutes his body with flesh of a sheep, now he wishes to pollute the water with his. This is a sight neither I nor Robyn wish to witness."

Albanroot looked from Elf to Horse and then to Pike. "Is that what horse-talk sounds like?"

"What do you mean?" asked Pike.

"Snorting, blowing and baying."

"Well, that sums up his personality, generally, but to me it sounds like he's talking, so you must be right."

"Ah, I think I understand now: the gift is within you and Elf. It is not the animals who talk your language; it is you who understands theirs."

"I doubt it, Albanroot. I can only understand these two. It's not as if I can yack with just any old beast. By the Gods, I could never have eaten that sheep if I'd had a conversation with it first.

"Now, I need to clean-up."

From his saddle bags on Horse's back, Pike pulled out a set of clothing which, while not exactly clean, was certainly cleaner than the stuff he was wearing. He also checked that his copy of the Great Book was safe.

The others left the pool and Pike stripped naked, hoping his skin wouldn't peel off with his clothes. It felt good to be rid of them: there were so many layers of grime on his outfit that it was practically impermeable. He had forgotten what it was like to have the breeze blow against his chest. Tentatively he dipped a toe into the pool of water and caught his breath.

Ice cold.

Back in Ooze it was rare to totally immerse one's self into a river or a stream unless it was a baking hot day, and that wasn't often. Today was not baking hot, it was merely warm. However, even Pike could smell how bad he was right then so, plucking up courage, he jumped in belly first. Spray flew everywhere, and he shrieked with the agony of the coldness. He stood up, realising that the water was fairly shallow; it barely reached his groin. The breeze against his skin chilled him even more, so he squatted back down. This time, his body fooled by the contrast, the water felt slightly warmer. He dipped his head under and scrubbed at the roots of his straggly hair.

When Pike surfaced he was surprised not to see the familiar flakes of dry skin that normally surrounded him in water. He rubbed the back of his hand against his chin. He was not yet in the habit of shaving, as his growth was too weak to bother about, so there were tufts of soft hair on his jawline and upper lip, but apart from that his skin was smooth. He rubbed the rest of his face, watching for the snowfall: nothing.

"Wow!" he yelped, loudly.

Pike's elation ceased when he heard someone chuckling. It sounded like a girl or a woman. He glanced around rapidly.

"Who's there?" he demanded.

The chuckle stopped. There was a rustling in the trees that was not caused by the wind.

"Show yourself," called Pike, wondering why he said that. He didn't know what he would do if an enemy was there, other than leap nakedly out of the water and run around in a panic.

"You're naked. What are you going to do if I do show myself? Leap out of the water and run around in a panic?"

"That's spooky, those were my thoughts exactly. Who are you?"

The rustling in the trees increased and Robyn flew out, landing on a stone next to the pool.

"It's only me!"

"Spying on me with no clothes on. What sort of sparrow are you?"

Pike could feel his face getting hot and knew he was blushing, but he didn't know why.

"You're over reacting a bit, Pike. I am, after all, only a sparrow. I'm sure you've bathed naked in the River Ooze in front of many other birds."

"Yeah, but none of them were on speaking terms with me."

"That should make no difference."

"Well it does. It's like stripping in front of a sister."

In as much as it was possible for a bird to have a facial expression, Robyn's face dropped.

"You look upon me as a sister?"

Pike shrugged. "I dunno. I haven't got a sister. But probably, yes."

"That's disappointing."

Pike wondered why it should be so, but said nothing. He washed his underarms, conscious of the bird watching him.

"What are you staring at?" he asked, somewhat exasperated.

"You. You've changed so much since we first met. It makes me proud to know I've helped you and that you've responded so well. Oh, and your face is no longer scaly and fish-like."

"Well, I know the flakiness has gone, but I don't see how the resemblance to a fish would have."

"I think," said Robyn, "that once the skin softened it stopped it from pulling around your lips and eyes, so they no longer bulge out like a trout."

"You reckon?"

"Yep. Let the water settle and see for yourself."

He did.

The transformation was quite remarkable, just as Robyn had said. His cheeks were healthy and soft, his eyes no longer bulged and his lips were no longer turned out and puffy.

"Cripes! Is that what a good moisturiser can do? Maybe I'll stand a chance with the fair maiden after all. I don't know how I'm going to get some more, though."

"We'll find a way Pike, because you're worth it."

He felt his face colour again.

"You really think so?"

"I do. You may no longer be a fish, but you'll be quite a catch for someone."

18: THE PACIFIC PLAINS

They stood atop a hill. The view was wondrous.

But it wasn't exactly a hill; it was more of a plateau. Some distance behind them were the trees surrounding the pool in which Pike had bathed, but in front of them the flat ground gave way to a steep slope that dropped away for many hundreds of adult feet. Pike could see a track, snaking its way down to the massive plain that lay below.

The ground down there, unlike where they stood, was brown and parched. The track carried on as an indentation through a dustbowl. It led to something in the distance that Pike couldn't quite make out. It was beyond his comprehension.

Cut into the plain was a large crater, out of which protruded five tall gleaming structures that shone in the strong sunlight. If he screwed his eyes up against the glare, Pike could just make out that these were like rectangular skeletons, many times taller than they were wide. At the top, forming a kind of 'T', was a second skeleton. Like the first, it was long. It stuck out for quite a distance in one direction, and much less in the other. Where the upright met the cross section, there appeared to be some kind of enclosure that reflected the sun. Pike was reminded of the clear shiny substance that Lord du Well used in his windows, and he wondered if this was the same. These five structures dominated the skyline and emphasised the size of the crater as, although huge, each looked isolated from the others.

"What is that place?" asked Pike.

"That," said Robyn, from Pike's left shoulder, "is the Pit of Zidor. The big flat area is known as the Pacific Planes."

"And those really tall things?"

"I believe they are called tower cranes."

"What do they do?"

"Not too sure, but if you look at the ends of the long arms, they have some kind of cable hanging down. Last time I flew around there, there was a man in each of those enclosures at the top, and they were moving things around on the end of the cables. They hang down into underground chambers."

Pike was amazed. "Hang on Robyn. You've been here before?"

"Yes."

"So you knew about all the hazards we'd face on the way?"

"Absolutely not! I knew of the Stinking Peat Bogs, and the one eyed winglekrats, and the worms, but not the other stuff."

"But you've been here, and you've been back. You must have known."

Robyn shrugged her wings. "No. I had serious help when last I was here."

"Moorlock?"

"The very one. He entrusted me with knowledge of this place so that I could bring you here. And here we are."

"Yes," said Elf. "Here we are. And there is our destination."

"Ah, my love awaits," sighed Pike, dreamily.

"Actually," said Robyn, "I've been meaning to talk to you about that."

"Not yet!" snapped Horse. "When we are closer to our journey's end, then you can tell him more. Remember how much he worried about the giant sabre-toothed worms when I told him about them?"

Pike huffed.

"I might have worried, but at least I got myself trained in combat when I found out, thanks to Elf, here. I'm surprised Lord du Well was happy to part with such a fine man."

"Du Well?" asked Albanroot. "He's not one of du Well's men."

Pike's jaw dropped. He could feel his mouth opening and closing, but no words came out.

"Pike," said Robyn, "You know I said you no longer resembled a fish? Well I wasn't lying, but right now, you're puckering-up like a guppy."

Pike breathed in deeply. Finally, words came out; he spoke to Albanroot, but his eyes were fixed on Elf.

"He must be one of du Well's men. He came with us from the Fort."

Elf said nothing; he continued to survey the area ahead of them.

"He's not," confirmed the shepherd. "I've lived at Fort du Well for many years and I'd have noticed a man of his size."

"Look, when I found out I was going to die, I asked you to identify for me the best swordsman in the outfit and to bring him to me. This is who you brought."

"That is so, but he is not one of du Well's men. He was sparring with the soldiers when I found him, and he was a superior fighter – they all said so – so I chose him for you."

"So if he isn't from Fort du Well, where is he from?" asked Pike.

"I don't know," said Albanroot. "Lucky find, though, don't you think?"

Pike did not respond. Elf must have heard the conversation, but he, too, remained silent.

"Who are you, Elf?" asked Pike.

Elf turned to him.

"A soldier of fortune. Nothing more than that."

"And what is one of those?"

"I sell my services to others who need a warrior."

"Sell? You mean for money?"

"Indeed."

"So you've come along to make a profit?"

"Why not? You are going to profit, are you not? You've come to win the heart of a fair maiden; that will be your reward."

"That, and to release Moorlock the Warlock from his mortal enemy. I think I deserve something for my trouble, and a little bit of love sounds good."

Elf grinned.

"In that place, young Pike, are riches untold, and I think that my reward lies there. I have helped you this far, I'll take whatever I want as payment, thank you."

"Riches? What use will they be to you? That money thing will never catch on, you know. If you need payment, come back to Ooze with me and my new love, and you can have your weight in watermelons."

The big man scratched his bearded face, thoughtfully.

"Hmm, tempting ... almost tempted ... nearly there ... No! I'll take my spoils from Zidor, if you don't mind."

"Well even if I did mind I could hardly stop you. But can we trust you? Why didn't you tell me about this before?"

"Seemed little point to it."

"But I thought we had become friends."

"We have, but that doesn't mean I can't be paid. What's it going to cost you, personally? Nothing! It's all down there, waiting to be taken."

Pike felt deflated. He really had trusted Elf, but the huge man had not been open and honest with him.

"I'm not sure that what's down there should be taken. Maybe that's what this is all about: maybe I'm supposed to stop that place being used."

Elf smiled broadly.

"If you have no idea what's there, why should you be worried?"

"I have a very uneasy feeling, that's all."

Horse spoke. "You are right to feel uneasy, oh heroic leader. Down there lies the path to the destruction of the world."

"I thought," said Robyn, "we weren't going to tell him anymore yet. You just said so."

"Tell me more! Now! I command it!"

"Calm down, Pike," said Robyn, softly.

"Calm down? Horse has just told me we're headed for somewhere that can destroy everything, and you want me to calm down?"

"Well it was worth a shot."

Pike mounted his steed and cleared his throat.

"OK. We have no choice but to trust Elf and pray that he doesn't just abandon us when we get to the Pit–"

"Ah-hem," Elf interjected. "That doesn't sound like trust; it's hope."

"Good, 'cos I hope we can trust you. I hope that when we get there you can help to complete my quest. I hope we can save one warlock and one maiden, not to mention my life."

Elf clapped his hands slowly.

"Well done, young master. A rebel-rousing speech, spontaneously made. I'm almost tempted to work for free."

"Fat chance. Let's get going before I chicken-out."

"You know," said Robyn, as they set off down the steep, zigzagging slope, "it's a fallacy about chickens being cowardly. They are some of the bravest birds I know."

"Don't be stupid," panted Horse, twisting around a boulder.

"I mean it. They live with humans all their lives and it almost always ends in grief; first they have their precious eggs stolen on a daily basis, then some brute turns up, breaks their necks, rips all their feathers off and cooks them over high heat. Yet still the remaining ones stay with the humans."

"That's nothing to do with bravery and everything to do with dumb!"

"If you ask me," said Pike, "it's about survival. We all take advantage of whatever we can. I don't detect much sympathy for the worms you gobble down, Robyn."

"Now, worms really are dumb," said the little bird. She was flying alongside them, circling, so as not to get too far ahead.

"So really dumb is good to eat?"

"Reckon so."

It took a long time to reach the base of the slope. When they did, Elf liberated several water flasks from Horse's saddle-bags.

"Two each for the humans. Horse, are you going to survive this trek with no further water?"

The sacred beast gazed up at the sun: it was afternoon and it was past its highest point.

"I should think so. If we are lucky there will be some along the way."

"I didn't see any from up there," said Pike.

"You know what?" said Albanroot, who had been extremely quiet since announcing that Elf was not from Fort du Well. "It would be nice to be included in the conversation, from time to time. I only get to hear half of it."

"Ah. Sorry. We were discussing Horse being able to get to the Pit of Zidor without water. I was just saying, I couldn't see any from up there."

"Well if you'd told me, I could have pointed out the cactus plants that grow around these parts. They are filled with liquid. Bitter, but strangely refreshing."

"I didn't see any plants," said Pike.

"They blend in with the colour of the earth."

"Amazing," said Pike, genuinely impressed. "How do you know these things?"

"I'm a shepherd. It's my job."

Pike looked around, but could still see nothing resembling a plant. Then he looked back the way they had come, straining his neck to see the top of the slope. Suddenly he saw them: two black dots, coming down the zigzag path.

"Erm, Elf? We're being followed."

"Have you only just noticed? She's been with us since Fort du Well."

"By the power of Adriarch the Sinner! You are full of secrets. When did you know?"

"Read my lips: she's been with us since Fort du Well."

"Ah!"

"But I didn't know it was she until the night after we had slain the worms."

"Right. Who is she? And who is she with? There are two black dots up there."

"Ooh! Me, me! I know this one!"

Pike turned to the excited voice. "Albanroot?"

"Yeah: me, me! It's Scarlet Deadnight, and her faithful hound, Rufus."

"By the gods! Am I the only one around here who doesn't know what's going on?"

"The only person," said Robyn. "I knew we were being followed, but I didn't know her name. I told Elf some while ago. Horse, on the other hand, had no idea."

"So how do you know, Albanroot?"

"Well, I don't. Didn't, rather. But when Elf said 'she', and that 'she' had been with us since Fort du Well, that left only one option."

Pike felt like he was being excluded from everything. "For goodness sake, this is my quest. You all keep telling me I'm the chosen one, but none of you trusts me with the truth."

Elf, standing alongside Horse, patted Pike on the knee. "Well, there seemed—"

"—little point. I know, I know," finished Pike. "Right, let's get on with this journey and you can all tell me what I don't know. Starting with who is Scarlet Deadnight."

*

"Scarlet," started Elf, trudging forward through the dust, "is a ruthless huntress: an assassin."

"What's an assassin?"

"Someone who kills for payment, or for a cause. She kills for both reasons."

Pike shifted in his saddle. He was sure his bum was beginning to blister.

"What's her cause?"

"Enjoyment."

"Oh."

"She's very professional: she can make it last for as long or as short a time as she chooses – but it's always her choice. Those whom she respects will not suffer too much at her hands, but if you have crossed her, or she thinks you are weak, she will draw it out for days on end."

"Sounds evil."

"Indeed," agreed Elf, "and when I used the word 'draw', I did so as a clever linguistic device, as in: to hang, draw and quarter."

"Meaning?"

"Hanging by the neck until almost dead; drawing out your innards while you are still breathing, and then chopping you into four parts. I'm assured that the last part is a blessed relief, though I've not tried it myself."

Pike gulped.

"Does she have any good points?"

"Absolutely," snapped Albanroot. "She's all the way back there and not catching us up very quickly."

Elf chuckled. "Perhaps that is her finest point. However, she is honourable, in a perverse sort of way. That's demonstrated by her dictum of a quick death if she respects you."

"I wonder how she feels about me."

"If she's seen half of what we've seen," said Elf, "you won't suffer for long if she does catch you."

"Thanks, I think."

They continued across the plain, stopping when Albanroot spotted a cactus or two at the side of the trail. On those occasions he would hack pieces off them and feed them to Horse to suck on. The beast spat them out when the moisture had gone.

Scarlet and Rufus remained as dots in the background. Pike couldn't tell if they were gaining ground or not.

Ahead of Pike and his group, the tower cranes loomed large. Even from that distance they dwarfed the landscape. They were semi-shrouded in a heat haze, but he could just make out the cables running from the tops of the towers to the end of the arms, and the long cables that disappeared into the pit itself. He was filled with wonder at the thought of what they were and who could have built them. All he had known before embarking on his journey was the low-grade yet functional building style of his village. Then he had been amazed at the futuristic design of Fort du Well, with its large palace and that transparent shiny stuff they used in the windows to stop the elements and allow light to enter, not to mention the thing he had used when he had needed a bush! But these tower cranes ... they were something else again.

Out loud, he said, "Who – what – could have built those things?"

Elf, trudging alongside Horse, replied, "I think there are a few things that Robyn and Horse must tell you. How about it, you two?"

Robyn, who had been hovering on thermal streams above them, landed on Horse's head and said, "Moorlock gave me instructions that I should only tell him when both Horse and I agreed."

"Hang on," said Pike, "Moorlock knew about Horse? How could he? You were sent to help me on my quest, then we captured and tamed Horse. He couldn't have known we'd do that."

Horse let out an explosive snort and whinnied in disgust.

"I am neither captured nor tamed! I am subservient to no one, and you had better remember that. I am here because I chose to be so. I fight for the greater good, for the benefit of our world. Moorlock knew I frequented Ooze and he knew that I was the only possible chance you had of getting this far."

"Did he also know of your pig-headed arrogance and self importance?" asked Robyn.

"Of course he did. He's Moorlock."

Robyn jumped off Horse's head, landing on the ground in front of him, causing them to stop.

"Well in my humble – if unworthy – opinion," said the bird, "I think it's time that Pike knew of the truth, oh great and sacred beast." Robyn finished by raising her left wing high in the air, sweeping her right wing across her chest and bowing in an overly dramatic gesture.

Albanroot, who had been trailing behind slightly, stepped forwards and stood next to Robyn, facing Pike. "This is all very confusing, Pike, sir. I know you and the two animals are talking, and I feel very left out. If I am to go the rest of this journey with you, I really need to know what's going on."

"That's fair, young master," said Elf. "However, translating the entire conversation might prove onerous. Do you still have the Great Book to hand?"

Pike dug into the saddle bag and withdrew the book. Elf took it from him and flicked through the pages rather rapidly. He grinned broadly, his amazingly white teeth gleaming in the sunshine.

"Ah. Here. Look." He passed the book back over to Pike and pointed at a page. The Great Book was open part-way through the chapter headed, *Concerning Spells and Hexes*. Elf pointed to a passage headed *Communincantation.*

"What, exactly, am I supposed to do with this?" asked Pike.

"Once, a long time ago, a very great magician used this incantation on me as payment for a favour I performed. I wanted a real payment, but he told me that one day it would come in very useful, and it would reward me in unimaginable ways. I couldn't argue with him, as he had protected himself with very strong magicks; had I tried to fight him I would have perished. For many years I wondered what he meant. Then you arrived at Fort du Well. I was passing through, between assignments, and I had fully intended to present myself to du Well as a hired soldier. But then I heard something: I heard these two critters talking to each other, and then to you.

"At first I thought I was going mad: I couldn't see any of you, but I could hear things in my head. I knew there was a horse and a bird involved, so I had to track you down. It wasn't difficult to find a trio such as you, in a place like Fort du Well."

Pike nodded slowly. "So what, exactly am I supposed to do with this?"

"I guessed that the incantation would be in this book. Recite it: give Albanroot the power to understand these two creatures."

"Don't be ridiculous," huffed Pike. "I have no knowledge of magicks. How could I possibly give Albanroot such a power?"

Elf grabbed Pike's arm and pulled the youth towards him. There was a look of stern intensity on Elf's face.

"You are The One, young master. You do have powers, but you don't know what they are. Now is the time to see what you can do." He let go of Pike's arm. Pike, in turn, sprang back into an upright position.

"For the hired help around here you seem very passionate about all this," said Horse.

"Passionate enough to ensure my payment. If all of us can understand each other we stand a better chance of success and I stand a better chance of winning my spoils."

"You're all heart," said Pike, dismounting from Horse. He looked at the page and tried to figure out what was written. "This isn't English."

"Incantations rarely are. Just follow the instructions and read it out word for word. That should work."

The instructions were simple enough: "Place right hand on subject's forehead; subject must kneel. Incant the words three times. Touch the persons or animals with which communication is desired. Incant the words twice. The incanter must cross the fingers of his left hand and genuinely hope it works. Doesn't seem a very precise way of doing stuff."

"It's ancient magick, Pike," scoffed Elf. "There's nothing precise about it at all. It's all down to power and hope."

"OK," said Pike, approaching Albanroot, his right hand outstretched. "Let's give it a try."

Albanroot knelt when Pike's hand touched him.

Taking a deep breath, Pike began.
"Icht nah alc tellitch montine argnithick …"

19: A SHORT LESSON IN HISTORY – BY HORSE

"In the beginning there was a vast civilisation.

"It was massive. Huge. Enormous.

"Nobody really knew what came before it, so everyone assumed that it was there from the beginning. It had been there for so long, no one could imagine that anything could have come before it, so it was assumed that the phrase 'In the beginning there was a vast civilisation' was a fact. But it was not.

"The people of this civilisation knew a thing or two about how things worked and they took full advantage of their environment. Every home used something called electricity, and this electricity was used to provide power (not magick power, but the stuff that powers things like lights, fires and things called TVs and PCs – no one really understands what a TV or a PC were, but they sure as heck had them, and they were powered by electricity). They also used stuff called petrol and oil, and they used these things to power carriages and carts that needed no sheep or hound to draw them; instead they used engines. So great were these engines that humans used to measure them in horse power. Invoking the name of the sacred beasts just goes to show how much power they must have packed: why else would they have made such a comparison?

"The petrol and the oil ran out. No one really knows why this happened, but it did. It was a sign of the perversity of humans that many of the sources of electricity were reliant on oil, so when petrol and oil ran out, so did much of the electricity. But humans are a resourceful breed: they moved on to something called fusion power.

"No one these days knows what fusion power was, but it was far more powerful than all of the gods and all of the sacred beasts put together. Fusion power was to be the saviour of mankind. It was an endless and cheap source of energy and now it meant that humans could have as many TVs and PCs (whatever they were) as they wanted.

"What happened next was horrible.

"The power that humans created was made by something called a reactor. Something caused one of the reactors to react badly, and before anyone knew what was going on, a whole load of other reactors did the same thing and mankind was almost completely wiped out. There were explosions and storms, and the planet got hot, and rumour has it that places like the Stinking Peat Bogs and this very plain on which we now walk were created by that disaster.

"For thousands of years, mankind tried to re-create itself from scratch. When technology died the ancient magicks re-manifested themselves after being buried in the psyche of humans for many thousands of years. As if from nowhere, manuscripts of great antiquity reappeared, detailing spells, hexes and incantations once thought lost forever. The balance of nature seemed to be restoring itself, and humankind appeared to be harmonising with its environment, treating it with respect and living as it should without excessive greed.

"But mankind craves hierarchy: most people yearn to be dominated by powerful overlords, whilst others yearn to be those overlords. Unlike we horses, you people need government and rules, regulations and higher and lower classes. People like Lord du Well built fortresses to protect themselves from their enemies – he didn't have any enemies until he advertised that he thought he did. Once the walls went up, the marketplace for artefacts from the vast civilisation of which I speak was opened up.

"Man needed forts and cities, then the cities and forts needed technology so that they could outdo each other and gain power – and this time I mean the sort of power that corrupts, where some men rule over others and expect those others to be totally subservient. Man is unique in this aspect, Pike: once a human tastes power over just one thing, he wants it over all. One village is not enough: he wants a town, then a city, then a whole continent. Finally, the world. Men who crave power such as this see it as their right, and one which they can abuse, whereas they should see it as a privilege, and a burden that they carry for the common good. Those who crave power have no right to it; only those who shun it should be given the gift – and they are rare creatures indeed.

"There is one man who already has mastered the magick arts, but who now craves that other kind of power. Rumour has it that he used his magicks to locate the lost city of Zidor, and that is what we see before us, in the pit. His minions work day and night in that pit, digging for technological artefacts that he can use to help him rule the world. It is from there that Lord du Well obtained many items that now sit in his fort."

Horse had spoken as the small team marched on towards the Pit of Zidor. The sun was lowering in the sky and they had made good progress. The two dots that were Scarlet and Rufus had gained some ground on them, but they were still only dots.

"This man," said Pike. "Is it Lord du Well?"

Elf roared with laughter. "That miserable little pipsqueak? He would never have mastered the magick arts: he hasn't the intelligence to master the art of wiping his own backside."

"But he has lots of stuff from the Pit: he showed me paintings of men and women on horseback, and asked me – well, more or less commanded me – to train his men to capture and ride horses in return for him supplying me with an army to reach my destination."

Horse whinnied. "A demonstration of his stupidity, Pike. First of all, he assumed that you had captured me and could train his men to do so, and secondly, you told him that you were coming here to win the heart of a fair maiden. He is so totally rubbish that it never occurred to him what you meant."

"Of course he did. He knew I was coming here to rescue Moorlock – that's why he provided the army – and to find the love of my life (I hope)."

"But that," said Robyn, once more sitting on Pike's shoulder, "is only what you thought you meant. Du Well could have put two and two together, but he is so dumb that he sponsored your journey when he should have been killing you. Afterwards, I assume, Scarlet Deadnight figured it out and tagged along to see if there was any danger of you succeeding. It must have looked like you'd fail, early on, but you proved yourself to be made of stern stuff. Doubtless, du Well would love to make a power play, but he wouldn't know where to start. Scarlet would run the show and probably double cross naïve Nairey at the first opportunity. "

"Will one of you please tell me what you are both talking about."

"The man who is excavating the lost city of Zidor is Daniel Fairmae," said Horse.

"Yeah, so?"

"So," said Robyn, "he's known as Dan and he's really ugly. All that exposure to powerful dark magick has taken its toll. As a joke, his minions reverse his name, so Dan Fairmae becomes Fairmae Dan."

"The best thing about humans is their use of irony," said Horse.

Realisation dawned on Pike, and he felt the blood drain from his face.

"You mean, the fair maiden whose heart I have come to win is a man?"

"Afraid so," said Robyn.

"But I'm not attracted to men."

"Even if you were, you wouldn't be to this one," said Horse.

Robyn continued, "You haven't come to romance him, you've come to win his heart."

"Eh?"

"You have to challenge him, win, cut out his still-beating heart and use it to free Moorlock."

20: PREPARING TO FIGHT

"Dan Fairmae … fair maiden … Dan Fairmae … fair maiden … kill Dan Fairmae … kill the fair maiden … rip out his heart …"

"Do you think he's ever going to stop saying that?" asked Horse.

"I doubt it," said Albanroot. "He's in a state of shock."

"Kill the fair maiden …"

"Frankly it's getting on my hooves. He's a hero, for goodness sake. What did he expect?"

"He's not just a hero; he's a reluctant one. What he expected was to be left alone to lead a simple life. He'll never let it go to his head. He's that rare kind of human you mentioned, who will never seek power and would see it as a burden. He will make a great leader because he doesn't want power at any cost. In fact, he doesn't want power at all. You can't expect him to be like that and be blasé about it."

"I know you're right, shepherd, but the repetition is making my mane tingle in a bad way."

They continued their journey across the plain, Pike still on horseback. Now the tower cranes were terrifyingly huge. With the sun lower in the sky it was possible for Pike to make out the shape of a man in the clear enclosure of the nearest one. He knew that if they could see this man, the man could see them. Would that person be able to tell Fairmae that strangers approached?

"Kill Fairmae: I have to kill Fairmae. Rip out his heart." He gesticulated with his hands, miming how he thought he would have to do it. Then he shuddered. How could he rip anyone's heart out? He couldn't kill another human being, could he? Killing giant sabre-toothed worms was bad enough.

Robyn swooped down from above and landed between Horse's ears. "Pull yourself together, Pike. We're nearly there, and you have some studying to do."

"I can't do it, Robyn. I can't kill a man."

"I'm sure you'll change your mind when he's trying to frazzle you with a spell or two. Anyway, these days there isn't actually much humanity about him. He's a little different, you might say."

"I don't understand why I should have to. Surely Moorlock is powerful enough to fight him? I'm just a boy with no powers at all. What can I do?"

Robyn shrugged. "You are The One. You have to do it. You have the power to do anything you feel is right. Moorlock is the most adept magician I know of, apart from Fairmae. You have to rescue him."

"Great, you know of only two powerful magicians, and I'm neither of them, and Fairmae is the better of the two. If Fairmae is so great, how can I defeat him?"

"You have right on your side. You are not corrupt. Even Moorlock, with all his powers over white magick, is tainted to some degree, but you are not. You've never wanted power; you still don't. I bet you never will. But the future lies with you. You must spend what little time we have left before reaching the Pit, studying the spells and hexes that will protect you."

"I'll never have time to remember what I need to know. We'll be at the edge of the pit soon; then what will I do?"

Elf spoke. He had been quiet since Horse had given his potted history of the world. "I have heard that warlocks use a special memory technique. Pass me the book, please."

Pike handed over his copy of the Great Book and Elf flicked through the pages. He stopped from time to time, apparently reading through some sections rapidly, muttering to himself.

"Ah, here you are! It's in the chapter about spells and hexes: an incantation to improve memory and learning." Elf passed the book back.

"Well that's great," enthused Pike. "We could all incant it and then read the spells and stand a better chance of—"

"No!" snapped Elf. "It doesn't work that way. Read the guidance notes at the foot of the page."

Pike looked at the bottom of the page and saw a footnote: *Memory Spell - for the exclusive use of those with the birthright. WARNING: Unauthorised usage may lead to loss of life or worse.*

"What does that mean?"

"It means you have to do it, we can't," said Elf. "You're the only one here with the power as your right from birth. No birthright, no usage of the memory spell – or any others, I'd wager."

"Why not the others?"

"Because they're all gobbledegook. Unless you read them directly from the page you'd never get the words out. Either that, or you'd need to spend several years memorising them."

Elf was right. The words of the *Communincantation* he had only recently spoken for Albanroot were lost to him.

"So if I just read out Ligt ra icht nah igbor abum dabnaba I'll immediately develop a super memory?"

Pike didn't hear an answer. Instead, he felt a sharp, splicing pain in his head, as he fell off Horse and onto the dry, dusty track. The pain shot through his skull from his forehead to his spine, causing his back to arch and his entire body to burn with agony. Memories flooded his mind at lightning speed. Birth: the glint of light, the screams of his mother's pain and the face of Gran, leering at him lovingly. First feed, and the comforting body odour of his mother. First steps: faltering, falling, crying. First words: "More melon!" Playing on the banks of the Ooze. Kids mocking him. Moorlock at the stone. His first melon harvest. The jibes from the villagers. Flaky skin. His brothers, uncles, cousins. Everything. Too much. His head would explode.

It didn't.

Pike's mind was suddenly clear: too clear … hauntingly so. He stood up slowly and deliberately, aware of the others watching him expectantly. Picking the Great Book up from the ground he said, "I remember my birth."

"I'm sure some things are forgotten for a purpose," said Albanroot. "Did it hurt?"

Pike nodded slowly. "A little … gave me a headache. Mum was a bit cut up, though." He slowly sank back down to the ground.

"What else do you remember?" asked Elf.

"I remember before I was born."

"Yuk," chipped in Horse.

"Not words. Just images in my head ... warm and wet and comforting. Tinged with pink. I remember everything else."

Elf frowned. "Everything else?"

"Hmmm."

"That's fantastic," said Robin, who was now perched on Elf's head.

"Not really …"

"Course it is," said Robyn, expectantly flapping her wings. "You'll be able to zip through the spells in no time."

"Some of my memories are really bad."

"Oh! Forget about them, they're all in the past. Just concentrate on the book – that's your future."

Elf plucked the sparrow from his head, snarling and baring his gleaming, white teeth menacingly.

"Shall I snap this annoying little creature's neck now or later?"

"Leave her alone, Elf. I could do without another bad memory to haunt me."

"Very well, young master."

Elf tossed Robyn into the air. She fluttered over to Pike and landed on his right knee.

"A bit tetchy today, isn't he?"

"I'd better get back on to Horse and read the book."

It didn't take long to memorise the protection spells, attack hexes, and the open the door and escape incantations, but Pike didn't feel any more confident afterwards than he had before. If he understood correctly – and he was sure he did – Fairmae was a magician of great magnitude and experience. Pike, on the other hand, was a melon farmer with a good memory, only recently acquired. He had read the spells but he had no idea what the words meant – all those ichts and nachts and ignatchtinchs were totally beyond him. In his mind he had ordered them into groups of attack, protection and escape. He knew that some would disable or harm an enemy, and some would shield him, but the actual effect of each was not explained on the page.

Oh well, he had gone into this whole affair blind, he might as well carry on that way, he supposed.

Pike, who had concentrated so hard on the words that he had been oblivious to anything else, put the book back into the saddlebag just as Horse drew to a halt. He silently dismounted and stood at the edge of a huge crater. Several hundred adult feet below sprawled a massive city. Its roads, emanating from under the bank of earth on which he stood, appeared deserted and its buildings, many of them tall rectangular towers, were covered in dirt or dust. Parts of the city were still under layers of earth, only partially excavated. The tower cranes were spaced across the area at even intervals, their thick cables slowly winding up or down. Even from that height, clearly visible at the side of a road leading into the city was an enormous sign in faded colour. The image was of a smiling girl-child, clothed in a bib-fronted red dress, and with blonde pig-tails and two missing front teeth, clutching a bunny rabbit. The rabbit didn't look real, somehow (for that matter, thought Pike, neither did the girl). In bold red letters below the picture were the words

Give your ears a rest!

Zidor Heavy Duty Batteries

They go on and on, so your child won't have to!

"What the heck does that mean?" asked Pike.

"I have no idea," replied Elf. "But it's the first thing of note they discovered when the excavation began, hence the name: the Pit of Zidor."

21: INTO THE PIT

The dots representing Scarlet and Rufus were considerably larger by the time the five made their way down into the Pit via another zigzagged path.

Pike was going to walk down, but Horse insisted otherwise: "I understand that the use of the magicks is exhausting, so you need to save your energy."

That didn't mean much to Pike: he was already exhausted and emotionally drained. If only he could have tried out the memory spell earlier in the journey, then he might have had time to recover from the shock of it.

They travelled mainly in silence; this pleased Pike, as it gave him some time to come to terms with remembering every fact of his life. Particularly difficult for him was the indignity of babyhood; the inability to carry out even the most basic task and having to rely on someone else (not often his mother, who was too preoccupied with styling her melon-skin bonnet to care about much else) to clean him up after he soiled himself. He knew what Albanroot meant when he had commented that some things are forgotten for a reason. Other things that bugged him included the bullying by those he thought were his brothers, but who may have been uncles; the wicked temper and wackiness of Gran, and his mother's general ineptitude as a mother. None of these memories had bothered him before because he had stashed them away in the back of his mind, but now they were burned deep into the front of his brain. He didn't suppose his life was much different from any other child raised in a village such as Ooze, but how many others had to recall every single detail with crystal-clear clarity?

As they neared the bottom, Pike wondered what had happened to all of the soil and debris that had been dug out of the pit.

"Ah, the wonders of magicianship," sighed Robyn. "Fairmae needed all the help he could get to excavate this area – it was too risky just to hex the soil away – but once it was dug up he was able to send it away in bulk. If we had tried to cross the Pacific Plains while the dig was still taking place, the chances are we would have been buried under the debris he hurled across it in all directions."

They moved on, reaching the bottom of the path in a surprisingly quick time. Looking over his shoulder Pike could see no sign of Scarlet having reached the edge of the pit.

"You're very knowledgeable for a bird," said Pike. Then something suddenly occurred to him. "I don't understand what I am supposed to do with Fairmae's heart," he announced.

Elf looked aghast. "Was there nothing in the book about restoration?"

Pike drew Horse to a stop and dismounted. The others also stopped.

"There was, but I thought it was about furniture or something, so I didn't bother reading it." He took the book out from the saddlebag and flicked through the pages until he found it and then showed it to Elf.

"Pointless showing me, young master: you're the one who needs to recite it."

Pike turned it back and just had time to glimpse the page before the book erupted into flames in his hands.

"Yeeieee!"

He dropped it onto the dirt immediately. Elf began stamping on it desperately, extinguishing the flames.

"I suppose that means he knows we're here, then?" said Pike.

"I guess so," replied Elf. "Did you read the restoration spell before the flames took hold?"

"Read it? I barely had time to glance at it."

"Let's hope that's enough."

"And if it's not?"

"I—I mean we—might cease to exist before too long."

Pike could hear the whine of the nearest tower crane. His view of it was partially obscured by the gigantic poster of the girl and the rabbit, but there it was, protruding from above, quite some distance behind it.

"Fairmae has a stronghold in the centre of the city. It stands on the edge of an old river bank," said Robyn, fluttering around as they made their way through the city. "The river used to flow right through the middle of this place. It was very wide."

"This whole place is huge," said Pike, a little breathlessly, "Ooze would fit into the Pit of Zidor hundreds of times over. How the hell did Fairmae get enough people to dig it all up?"

"A time spell," replied Elf. "He's a bad man, that's for sure. He won quite a few battles in the last few years and enslaved hundreds of captives. It is rumoured that he hexed all of them so that they worked in a time loop. They dug for only two years in our time, but it was forty for them. Most are dead from old age or over work."

"Nice fellow. How can I compete?"

Robyn answered. "You can't, but you have a pure heart. He can't cope with that. It's his weakness. He does what he does for his own selfish ends, but you actually have nothing to gain for yourself by fighting him."

"But I came here for selfish reasons: I was going to win the heart of a fair maiden, remember? I certainly do, along with everything else."

"Come off it," snapped Robyn. "You were the saddest specimen of a young man I'd ever seen, and you knew that. You never really thought you'd get the girl, even if there was one. The only reason you came along was because it was your destiny."

"I suppose."

The buildings they walked past varied in height from low-level, flat-roofed shops with one story, to tower blocks with twenty or more. All bore a patina of dark brown from the soil that once encased them, and some of the buildings, especially the taller ones, showed signs of structural damage. Some of them were separated by narrow alleyways, while others had large open areas between them. Strange signs hung over doors and windows – *DipDip Donut*; *The Majestic Burger House*; *Lolly's Diner & Strip Club – You eat, they strip*; *Rack 'em Up Pool Billiards & Snooker Club.*

"People used to live here?" asked Pike, almost lost for words.

"Live, work, play," said Elf.

"I'm not surprised it all went bad for them. No fields," said Horse.

"I don't see much in the way of grazing land for their sheep," observed Albanroot. "They did have sheep, didn't they?"

"Looking at that, I'd say so." Elf pointed to a building with a large window. Inside it was a counter and various things Pike thought might be used for cooking. A long skewer, attached to metal plates at the top and the bottom stood upright in front of some kind of metal device that had eight square grills attached to it. The sign above the window read: *Kypros Gyros – Doner, Shish and Adana Kebabs made with the freshest lamb. Chicken also available.*

The windows of the buildings were filled with that clear substance Pike had seen at Fort du Well and on the tower cranes. Many of the windows were cracked, though, and some were broken. He touched the sharp shard of one and recoiled as it dug into his shin, drawing blood.

"What is this stuff?" he asked.

"Glass," said Robyn.

"Well why would anyone want it? It's dangerous."

"Yeah, don't I know it? I lost count of the amount of times I banged my head when Moorlock first sent me here. One minute I'm flying through the air, the next I'm having to stuff my brain back into my skull. Bloody brutal!"

They continued through the dusty streets, with Pike marvelling at the variety of building styles.

"What does Fairmae want?" asked Pike.

"Power," replied Elf.

"But if he's so powerful already, why does he want more?"

"He's corrupt, plain and simple. There's a world of difference between powers of goodness and the dark powers he indulges in. Good people do good things for goodness' sake – these things can be simple and rewarding in their own right. People like Fairmae … well, they become intoxicated with greed and power. Just being evil and nasty to a few poor souls is never enough; they need to dominate the whole world. They want to strip the barriers between this world and another they believe exists, one where total corruption is the order of the day. In the times before the New Dawn, that place was known by various names – Hell, Hades, the Underworld, the Demon Realm. It was thought that if the barriers were broken down, actual demons – creatures of total evil – would break through into our world and those who brought this about would be rewarded by the demons."

Pike pondered this for a while.

"Two things come to my mind. Actually, loads of things are coming to my mind, but I'm trying to ignore my memories. First of all, he must know we are here – he burnt the Great Book – so why hasn't he done anything more to us? Secondly, what the heck is he doing, digging up this old city? How's that going to help him?"

"First off," said Elf, "he must think that meeting you face to face is going to amuse him. As for what he's doing here, well that's a mystery."

"Not so much," said Horse. "Technology: the ancients used it to destroy their world and it's taken thousands of years for the Earth to recover. I suggest he wants to use it to do a more complete job."

"So what does he want with Lord du Well? I can't see why he would have paired up with him."

Horse answered again. "He needs friends as well as slaves: people who follow him willingly. Maybe he wants them to worship him, once he becomes all powerful."

"You can ask him soon, when you meet him," said Robyn, landing on Pike's shoulder after a period of flying around. "We're just about there."

The building stood on a bank maybe one hundred or so adult feet opposite. In a strange, coincidental juxtaposition, from where Pike stood it appeared to be flanked by two of the tower cranes, giving the impression that they were holding it up, but in reality they were a considerable distance behind it. The exterior was impressively wide. Tall columns held up a portico that ran the entire width of it. At its centre was a gabled roof, held up with even taller columns. On the fascia of this gable was a frieze showing a battle between men on horseback and foot-soldiers in armour. Grand windows, every one apparently with perfect glass, adorned the building from one end to the other, showing it to be five stories high. At ground level, directly below the frieze, was a massive pair of wooden doors; they were closed. The name of the building had been carved into the stonework above the door: City Hall. Pike took note that out of all the buildings they had seen, this was the cleanest and in the best state of repair.

"So, that's Fairmae's palace, is it?" he asked, climbing down from the saddle.

"Yep," confirmed Robyn. "All we have to do is cross this dried up riverbed and we'll be there."

"Yes … then all I have to do is break down those doors, search through the entire building, do battle with possibly the most powerful man ever to exist, and rip out his heart. Should be simple enough, for a melon farmer like me."

Elf placed a hefty arm around Pike's shoulder and drew him close. "You sound far from convinced, which is a good sign. It shows you are not over confident about victory."

"No: it shows I am extremely confident – of losing!" He could feel his bile rising as he continued. "By the gods! How the hell did I get into this situation? You reckon the future of the entire world rests on my shoulders? Have you even seen my miserable, puny little shoulders? Have you? I've seen burnt twigs that fill me with more confidence. Robyn's shoulders are broader than mine."

"Don't be silly," chirruped the little bird.

"Well they are, comparatively. I'm damned if I shouldn't just fall onto the end of Elf's sword and save Fairmae the hassle of killing me."

Elf grinned. "He won't find killing you a hassle. The fact he's allowed you to get this far relatively unharmed is testament to the fact he's looking forward to killing you. He'll relish the opportunity. It'll strengthen him if he wins."

"By Holy Hearne: did you and Robyn go to the same school of motivational speaking? If that was intended to give me confidence it failed. Total and utter crap, the lot of it."

"I'm not trying to instil confidence; I'm telling you the reality. He's looking forward to meeting with you, he really is. He wants to kill you slowly and painfully, spit on your rotting corpse, devour your soul, dance on your grave and use the extra power to break down the barriers to the demon world. But he won't succeed. You still have a choice young master. Either you turn around and walk away, or you go and fight him."

"Walking away sounds less painful."

Horse snorted. "Not so. If you turn back, he'll seize on your weakness and he'll still do all that Elf says. But he'll win for sure. Whichever way you decide to play it he may win, but why make it easy for him? You could weaken him if you fight – give the next challenger an extra chance. You will suffer equally if you turn away or if you go and fight. In fact, he may reward cowardice with extra suffering."

Pike sighed.

"Albanroot: do you have an opinion?"

"Yes, I do. I'd hate to see you suffer. If you turn away I'll have viewed the consequences, but if you go and fight him I will be out here and I won't see a thing. Plus you might beat him."

"Thanks for that. Just as inspiring as Elf, you are. OK. I'd better be prepared to fight."

22: IN THE HALL OF THE MONSTROUS THING

The sun lowered behind them as they crossed the dried riverbed. To Pike, City Hall, already a sizable edifice, seemed to magnify tenfold as he drew nearer.

It's just my imagination, he thought.

No it's not, Robyn thought back to him. *It is getting bigger. I think Fairmae is doing it, to unsettle you.*

Hell, it's working!

"Is it just me, or can we all hear Pike and Robyn thinking to each other?" asked a bemused Albanroot.

"It's all of us," said Elf. Then: "Oi! I thought you were staying on the opposite bank to wait for us."

"I was going to, but then I thought, what the heck, I might be useful."

"Or you might get in the way."

"Of course, but I would seek to do that in a useful manner. Anyway, if we can all hear their thoughts, why don't we just talk out loud?"

Because, thought Robyn, *someone might hear us.*

Right, I understand. Can you hear me thinking?

Yes.

Everything?

No, thought Pike. *We can only hear what you want us to hear. We're not mind readers, you know.*

Good. That makes me feel better.

The river bank in front of City Hall was sheer, but it was encased in stone and a flight of steps led up from what would have been the water level. Elf lifted Pike up on to the bottom step and then did the same with Albanroot.

This is where I stop, thought Horse to the others. *No gentle slope, like there was on the other side.*

Pity, thought Elf. *I will miss your pessimism when we're inside.*

Don't worry: I'll be thinking doom-laden thoughts, just for you.

At once, Pike was overcome with emotion

Horse! I never said goodbye.

Now's your chance.

From up here?

By the gods, snapped Elf's thoughts. *Come back down and get it over and done with.*

Pike jumped down from the step, stumbling as he landed.

I shall think of you always in that position, thought Horse.

Yeah, because you put me in it, mostly.

Pike jumped up and threw his arms around Horse's neck, clinging on as if his life depended on it. Sobbing, he whispered, "If we never see each other again, just remember it's been an honour to have known you and to have ridden on your back."

"If we ever do meet again, don't squeeze my neck so tightly, OK?"

"It's a deal." He let go of the beast and rubbed a tear from his eye with his sleeve.

"Now you have a dirty streak on your face, idiot!" chuckled Horse.

"It's comments like that that I'll miss."

"Not for long. You be out in no time at all."

Elf lifted Pike back onto the step and then hoisted himself up. Horse helped by pushing the big man's bottom up with his head, and Pike and Albanroot helped by taking his hands. Robyn, meantime, was reconnoitring City Hall, flying to and fro and perching on windowsills, apparently randomly. She met them as they reached the top of the twenty stone steps leading up to ground level.

What's going on in there, little one?

I really don't know, Elf. Fairmae must have blocked all views into the place with a spell.

I see. Pike, think hard. What's going on inside?

How should I—oh! Pike stopped suddenly, pressing the fingers of both hands to his temples. *There's a huge entrance hall beyond the door. Maybe twenty or so people in there with weapons. Some are holding things I've never seen before – like a crossbow, with no cross.*

"Rifles," snarled Elf out loud.

What's rifles? Albanroot asked.

High powered weapons from the machine age. Some of them can kill a hundred men in one go. You pull the trigger like you do on a crossbow, but loads of tiny missiles fly out of the end. I'm surprised that even Fairmae would stoop so low as to use them.

Is that what advanced civilisations call progress? Albanroot asked.

Oh, they progressed much farther than that.

Can Fairmae hear our thoughts? wondered Pike.

No, thought Elf, only if you aim them at him. *In this group we are addressing each other with no restrictions, but if I were to think only to Horse –*

Pike suddenly stopped hearing Elf's words.

Horse says good luck, continued Elf.

They walked towards the massive wooden doors. Now they were closer Pike could see that the doors were highly ornate, with carvings of leaves around their outer edges. The wood was dark and scarred from being buried for goodness knew how long, but the hinges – enormous metal things – appeared to have been recently greased.

A large keyhole stared at Pike from halfway up the right hand door, taunting him. He glared back at it defiantly, screwing up his eyes a little for better focus.

Still just a fish-faced waste of space.

That thought pattern did not sound familiar. Pike knew how his comrades' sounded in his head: this was more coarse; malevolent, almost.

What are you doing? Elf's thoughts pulled him up short. He realised he was stepping closer to the door, to the keyhole, to that voice. He was closer than three adult feet from it.

There's a voice. It insulted me.

And drew you right in! Use your head, youth. Fairmae will entrance you in a trice if you let him.

The keyhole is staring at me. What should I do?

You read the Great Book: you tell me.

OK, I think I have an idea.

Pike took four paces backwards and raised his arms out to the side, holding them at shoulder height. Composing his thoughts, drawing on an inner strength that he didn't know existed, he began to incant:

"Acht nach ig bode la—" the door shook "—iche nagt—"

"Er – before you do that, don't forget to take this," yelped Elf, holding out the container of moisturiser.

"Elf, I'm a bit busy right now. Lacht ist nagh licht—"

"You need it. Take it."

"No. Sod the skin problem – it won't hurt me when I'm dead. Lay nah diddt nacght liber estos—" the wood around the lock began to splinter.

"I said take it, and don't forget to moisturise."

Pike stopped. The splintering stopped.

"You don't get to say that. Moorlock says that."

"Just take it, young master. Please."

Pike didn't know what to think. Surely, Elf couldn't be … no that was stupid. Elf was too big, too young, not obnoxious enough.

"Where would I put it? The container is too big for a pocket."

"Just hold on to it. You don't need to put your arms out like that anyway – that's for bedtime stories."

Pike took the box from Elf, realising it would be less hassle if he did so. He could dump it inside once the doors were down.

"OK. Acht nach ig bode la—" the door shook "—iche nagt—"

This time Horse interrupted: *Scarlet Deadnight alert. Here in five minutes.*

"Elf, go and deal with her. I have to get this door open. Now."

Horse watched them disappear over the top of the stone bank and waited. He wondered what he could do if and when Scarlet showed up. Maybe he could delay her long enough to let Pike into City Hall. When he sounded the alarm to the others it was meant as an early warning, not a plea for help.

But Scarlet appeared far more quickly than any human being should. Barely having time to utter a prayer to his ancestors, Horse reared up on his hind legs and kicked out with his forelegs.

Scarlet, her sword drawn, lunged towards Horse's belly, screaming. Suddenly Elf was there – the clash of his blade against hers being the first indication. Rufus snapped at Horse's legs, his sharp teeth menacingly close.

Whinnying, Horse leapt over Rufus and galloped away, sharply turning and doubling back, charging at the dog. Rufus looked confused, then terrified, then angry. Teeth again bared, drool pouring from the corners of his mouth, he lurched towards Horse's front legs, head at a sideways angle so he could grab hold with his powerful jaws.

Just as those teeth were about to make contact, Horse again raised up on his hind legs, dropped back down, and smashed his fore hooves onto the hound's spine.

Rufus howled in agony, but he wasn't finished yet. Getting up, spinning around under Horse's belly, he latched his jaws onto the rear of one of Horse's fetlocks, just above the hoof. Horse shrieked with the unexpected pain: it was worse than any he had known.

Horse kicked his front legs around viciously, trying to shake off the hound. It occurred to him that his life was about to end.

Elf responded to Horse's warning as soon as Pike told him to.

He ran down the steps and jumped the remaining distance to join Horse.

Scarlet and Rufus materialised from thin air just as Elf launched himself from the bottom step. Hell, she'd come up in the world.

The huntress lunged at Horse's belly with her sword held out before her. She had no chance to do damage, as Elf's own blade clashed with hers, deflecting it from the sacred beast's belly. He was aware of Rufus barking loudly and of Horse fighting the hound. Right now he had to deal with Scarlet, no matter what the cost.

"Neat trick, Scarlet. Where'd you learn that?"

He swung his sword aggressively, knocking her blade to the side. She recovered well, parrying and lunging towards him.

"I picked it up along the way," she panted, fighting off Elf's attack. "Who the hell are you?"

"Bet you wish you knew."

Elf kicked out at Scarlet's knee cap, the sole of his foot merely brushing her skin as she scuttled backwards.

"Actually, I'm not that bothered."

She swung her blade as if to chop off Elf's head: he jumped back deftly, raised his sword and deflected the blow in one fluid manoeuvre.

"Just let me get to the kid and the rest of you can walk away."

Elf lunged for the attack, narrowly missing her chest when she sidestepped, spun around and ended up behind him. Elf turned, twisting his knee. He grimaced, but tried not to let it show.

"That kid is the future," he grunted, on guarding before his next advance. "Why would I give you the future?"

Elf attacked, altering his cadence to confuse her.

"He has no future, big guy. You must realise that."

Scarlet counter attacked, dodging Elf's well measured swings and lunges. The crash of blade upon blade left Elf's eardrums ringing. Over the top of that ringing came the shrill whinnying of Horse. Having successfully reposted Scarlet's attack, he glanced over to see Rufus latching onto the beast's fetlock.

"Your dog's dying!" he yelled.

Scarlet was thrown off guard momentarily. It was enough for Elf to lunge again, this time driving his blade between her breast plate and shoulder. A jet of bright red blood spurted from the wound. She dropped to her knees, a look of surprise on her face.

Now, to save Horse.

"What should *I* do?" demanded Albanroot.

"Stay here and help anyone who comes out."

"Help them? They are the enemy."

"Fairmae is the enemy, they are enslaved to him. Now shut up and let me get these doors open."

He took a deep breath and began again. He wished Elf was with him, He also hoped that he had beaten Scarlet and saved Horse. The doors quaked under the barrage of incantation that emanated from Pike's lips.

"… lath nimt ignoghtable ist lakht …"

The wood around the lock splintered.

" … acht lothe est neegraboid …"

The door rattled and made slight progress inwards.

"… zergh labth nicht lacht. Gathaway, gathaway, GATHAWAY."

They burst inwards, as if smashed by a battering ram.

"Great work," congratulated Albanroot. "Be careful in there."

"And you out here," replied Pike.

Not stopping to look back at his friend, he walked into the entrance, aware that lots of men with those rifle things awaited him. He silently recited a shielding incantation. As with many of the protection spells he had read in the Great Book, it was designed to work by stealth and required no words to be uttered out loud.

Almost as soon as his second foot was over the threshold, there came the deafening clatter of repetitive gunfire from Fairmae's slaves with their weapons.

Bullets ricocheted from Pike's personal shield. He could feel the force of their impact, but no pain. In the gloom of City Hall's innards he saw the flashes from the gun barrels, and realised just how evil these things were.

"Lay down your weapons," he yelled over the cacophony of shooting, "or I shall have to remove them from you."

Almost immediately the gunfire stopped.

"See: that was easy. You can't harm me, and I don't want to harm any of you. Come on out and place your rifles in front of me.

He counted nineteen riflemen, as one by one they came out from behind upturned cabinets, tables and chairs, the barrels of their rifles still smoking. They wore little more than rags and all appeared dirty. Every one of them had a deeply lined face, and eyes that hinted at the unspeakable horrors they had endured.

"I'm here to release you from Fairmae. Beracct ests night alm nocht. Put down the rifles and go outside. My friend will look after you."

There was a vague murmur of acceptance from the men. They laid their weapons at his feet. One by one they filed past him, distrustful expressions on their faces.

That was when the bullet hit his right arm.

The shot was unexpected. Surely, all the men had surrendered? Then he realised that his pre-vision into City Hall hadn't been so clear: Twenty or so, he had surmised.

It was only a graze, but it stung badly, and blood trickled down his right biceps.

A weak spot in your armour, you insignificant little worm.

Pike knew it was Fairmae's voice inside his head.

Your spells aren't strong enough to save you from me, the voice continued.

"I'll give them a try," replied Pike.

I have more than two hundred years of practise under my belt: you only read a book, and now it's gone. Who's the stronger of the two?

"A very good question," Pike answered, carefully examining the foyer of City Hall for a lone gunman. "But if you're so great, why am I still alive?" He saw the merest hint of smoke rising from behind a rather ornate bureau that was lying on its side near to the exotic sweep of a balustraded flight of stairs.

Because I choose to torment you first.

"What are you going to do, bore me to death?"

Pike stepped forwards slowly and rechecked. Yep: smoke, highlighted by the rays of the setting sun as they shone through the busted doorway.

You speak stupidly, for one who is so outclassed. Show some respect for your elders and betters, and I might spare you from some of the suffering I have planned.

"I'd rather eat my Gran's cooking than show you respect. She's an awful cook, my gran."

Why waste energy by flapping your lips: communicate as I do.

"Why? So you can violate my brain and read my thoughts? If I let you in that far, who knows where you'll stop."

You're a bright lad, for an idiot.

"Rectatum oblivio nagistier!"

The bureau flew up into the air with a reverse spin and exploded. The splinters showered down on both Pike and a bewildered child who had been hiding behind it. Next to the child was a rifle.

"Did you use that thing against me?" asked Pike, softly.

The child, a young boy who looked to be no more than nine years old, nodded. Like the men, he was clothed in rags.

"I reckon you must be easier for him to control than the grown-ups. Come on, give me your hand." He reached out and the boy scampered backwards on his bum, stopping at the foot of the stairs.

"Seriously. I won't hurt you." Pike smiled at the kid. "You don't want to stay under Fairmae's thrall, do you?"

"Are y-you The O-One?" stuttered the boy, his high pitched voice wavering.

"So every one keeps telling me. Personally, I'm not convinced, but no one else seems to be doing this, so maybe I am. Come on."

The boy cautiously rose and accepted the outstretched hand. It was then that Pike realised he was still holding the container of moisturiser in his other.

"Listen: outside is a very good man named Albanroot. He's a shepherd. He'll look after you while I finish off in here. And could you take this out with you?" He held out the container.

"Does the shepherd have his flock with him?"

"Only if you count the men you were with."

"Thank you, Mr The One. I'll go and join them."

The boy started to walk away.

"Hold on. What about this?" Pike held out the container again.

"Don't be a silly-billy, Mr The One. I can't take the holy oil from you."

"Holy oil? It's moisturiser."

"They say the holy oil has magical healing properties, so maybe it's that as well."

"Who are they, and when did they say it?"

"It's written in the Great Book."

"But I've read the Great Book, and it says nothing of it."

The boy huffed. "Well maybe you had the abridged version. We learned from the full version and it says that The One – you – shall be anointed."

"Ah, yes, that was in my copy, but I don't know what it meant."

"I think it means you rub it on, or something. And if you're that special you'd be rubbing on holy oils, not just any old crap."

"Hmm, I see your point."

The boy grinned. "Good. I'll go and join the rest. Good luck, Mr The One."

There was a fluttering in the air, directly overhead, and the familiar voice of Robyn sounded in Pike's head. *Don't let Fairmae know I'm here. Don't acknowledge me in any way. Walk up the stairs and you'll find Fairmae on the top floor.*

Pike started the climb.

Elf's blade severed the hound's spinal cord when he drove it into its neck. Horse felt the jaws involuntarily tighten in spasm, and then slacken. The searing, burning pain was at once replaced with the dull throb of a bony injury. Blood seeped from a wound on his left fetlock.

"Close call," said Elf. "Can you walk OK?"

"Indeed it was, and indeed I can, I thought I was dog meat. Perhaps, if Pike succeeds, you humans can repay it in kind and feast on its bones. The will be no disdain from me."

"A tempting thought," said Elf, turning to look at Scarlet. "Damn! She's gone. I thought I'd killed her."

Albanroot didn't know what to do when he heard the gunfire, so he ducked down low and hoped it would stop: it did. He had no clue as to what to do when nineteen men came out of City Hall and walked towards him, pleading expressions on their faces. All he could do was offer soothing words and sing to them the *Song of the Lonely Shepherd.*

There was one more shot, and shortly afterwards a small boy came out and walked towards him.

"Mr The One said you'd look after us," said the boy, who then threw his arms around Albanroot's legs and hugged them, crying.

"I will," said Albanroot.

As he spoke these words, Elf bounded up the steps.

"Did you see the woman run past?" yelled Elf, running towards him.

"No, just these men and this boy."

"By Adriarch, where the hell has she gone?" Elf jabbed his sword at the stone paving in frustration, causing the newly released men to flinch. "And

Pike: is he inside?"

"Yes. He just freed this lot."

"Keep a look out for Scarlet Deadnight. She could kill all of you in the blink of an eye. I'm going in," yelled Elf running towards the open doors.

Although unhappy with the thought of the Huntress being at large, there was nothing other for Albanroot to do than to carry on his melancholy ballad.

On the second floor, Pike had to stop. A woman stood before him, her cheeks dirty and streaked with fresh tears. She was dressed in a black, hooded robe and had dark, greasy hair drawn back over her ears. Cleaned up she might have been pretty, but in that state, thought Pike, she looked wretched.

Pike walked across the galleried landing. As he approached her she spoke: "He has my baby." She sounded as pitiful as she looked.

"Where?" Pike asked.

The woman raised her hand to the side and pointed out over the railing. He followed the direction of her finger and was horrified to see a baby, no more than a few weeks old, levitating in the centre of the massive chasm that formed the space above the foyer. Pike caught his breath and grabbed the railing, his knuckles whitening. He looked up and down for any visible support, but there was none. All the landings above were as this one – galleried, overlooking the foyer. There were no strings, no ropes, no secret platforms.

His attention was drawn back to the woman when he heard her gasp. His heart almost stopped. She was now leaning back at an angle with a dagger held across her throat, as if some invisible fiend were holding her there. Behind the dirt on her face, her complexion paled to near transparency. She was uttering something that sounded like a prayer to Hearne.

Save the baby or save her? asked the voice in his head.

The baby started to bounce up and down, as if being thrown by a happy parent – except this parent was invisible and floating a good twenty adult feet above the ground.

Come on, Pike: save the baby and leave the mite motherless, or save mum and let her watch her baby die. Your choice.

Robyn, what can I do?

Save the baby. No! Save mum. No! I don't know.

"Stop playing, Fairmae," yelled Pike. "It's me you want to punish, so leave them alone."

But this is so much fun. This is how I'll make you suffer. Save one. You choose.

His eyes darted from mother to baby and back again. The baby would never know its mother, but she would always remember the baby's death. But who would care for the child?

He couldn't think of that now. He stepped towards the railings, ready to hurl an incantation at the child to deliver it safely to him. He knew that at his first utterance, Fairmae would kill the mother; that the dagger would slice open her throat and she would die in agony.

With a tightly knotted stomach, Pike scanned his extensive memory for the words, half wanting not to remember them for fear of making the wrong decision. He cast his eyes downwards – and saw something. Quickly he turned away from the child.

"Vastae ninckthampro estsus!" screeched Pike.

Three things happened: the baby dropped downwards, the blade flew away from the woman's throat, and the voice of Fairmae rang loudly within Pike's skull.

You killed the baby: you killed the baby! Woo-HOO! You killed the baby. No longer pure!

Another voice rattled Pike's brain – Elf's. *What in the name of Adriarch is going on? Babies falling out of thin air?*

You caught it?

Of course I caught it.

Pike's knees weakened with the relief. Then he noticed that the woman was hysterical and screaming. She was on her knees, crying, "My baby, my baby. You killed my baby."

Pike reached out to her.

"Your baby is safe. Go and get it."

She wailed on, oblivious to Pike's words.

"Really: he's safe. Go get him. Downstairs. Now."

He took hold of her shoulders and shook her. The woman stopped wailing enough to sob and ask, "But how?"

"Well," said Pike, confidently, "you stand up, dry your eyes, and walk down the stairs. It's easy enough."

She means, how is he safe, you nerk! thought Robyn.

"Oh! Right. He's been saved by my friend down there. He caught him. Go and get your baby. Please."

The woman stood up and said, somewhat doubtfully, "Are you saying this just to get me out of the way?

"No," replied Pike, perturbed by her tone.

"Because if you are lying to me, I'll be right back up here to find that dagger and use it on you!" She turned and swept away, her cloak billowing behind her.

"Don't mention it," said Pike. "Any time. Just glad I could help."

Think you're smart, Pike? Think you got one over on me?

Pike didn't stop to reply. Instead he launched himself at the next flight of stairs, running up them two at a time. In his left hand he held the moisturiser, with his right he clutched at the banister to hoist himself up as he ran. He reached the third floor and jumped on to the landing. Suddenly there was no floor. He felt himself falling.

Elf handed the baby over to the woman. She showed no more gratitude to him than she had to Pike. Nonplussed, he shrugged and headed to the flight of stairs.

"Where do you think you're going, big boy?" asked Scarlet.

Elf turned around to face her, drawing his sword rapidly.

"I thought I'd take a look around upstairs. Thought I might move in."

"Come on, big chap. Leave that little pipsqueak to Fairmae. You and me could be partners: you're a hell of a fighter." Scarlet's sword was also drawn and was held on guard.

"Not as good as I thought. You should be dead." His blade met hers with a crash.

"Maybe a piece of me died." She hit back, parrying.

Elf could see the blood on her shoulder where he had wounded her earlier. Surely she must be weakened?

"You heal well," he shouted, feinting to the right but attacking to the left.

"I do, but this time, it's to the death!"

"To the death, indeed," agreed Elf, his voice a coarse rasp as he forced his blade into Scarlet's throat.

23: DON'T FORGET TO MOISTURISE

Pike, why have you stopped?

I'm falling!

Pike squeezed his eyes shut tightly; his stomach dry heaved with the sensation of free fall.

No you're not, you're standing still.

He realised Robyn was right when he didn't smash against the ground. He shook his head and opened his eyes. There was no floor, but there was no falling: he was standing on air, and the air was where the floor should be.

I don't understand.

It's a trick. He's getting weak and this is the best he could do. The thing with the baby was supposed to finish you. If either one had died you'd have felt your innocence had been lost and you couldn't have faced him. Total rubbish, of course, but that's how it would have affected you.

So if I just carry on walking in mid-air, I'll get the rest of the way, will I?

Yes.

Why can't I see you?

I'm with you, that's all that matters.

He walked on, concentrating on the fact that there was a floor, despite appearances. The next flight of stairs was trickier – the treads were also invisible. On the fourth floor he was confronted by a solid landing, a disembowelled goat and an indescribable stench. The goat was strapped upside-down to a post that was wedged between floor and ceiling. Its entrails dangled down over its chin, dripping slowly onto the wooden boards.

The goat blinked.

This isn't real, this isn't real, this isn't real, Pike repeated.

Actually, Robyn thought to him, *this part is. But it shows how desperate Fairmae is now. He's resorting to ancient voodoo.*

What's voodoo?

Dirty magick. Very dark. Born of desperation. See where the blood drips?

Pike looked at the floor. A circle was painted there, maybe four or five adult feet in diameter. Inside it was a five-pointed star. The blood dripped centrally on to it.

That's a pentacle. Fairmae will be standing inside an identical one on the next floor up, directly above. The power down here will prevent you from reaching inside the circle upstairs.

Great, how do I get to him?

That's for you to figure out. Just try not to get blood on you when you go past that thing. It might taint you.

Pike edged towards the goat. There appeared only just enough room to squeeze between it and the delicate looking balustrade (the only thing between Pike and a four story drop). Cautiously he turned sideways and started to side step to get past. The smell was even more awful this close-up. Flies had attached themselves to the carcass and they made low buzzing noises.

He had just reached the other side and was heading for the next flight of stairs when he heard a rustling noise behind him. He turned. The goat's neck was arched back; the animal was staring at him. Its blood-drenched chin moved and it spoke.

"You can't get to the fair maiden, you know? He's invincible."

Pike's insides shuddered, but he was determined not to show his fear. "The opinion of a dead goat means so much to me."

"You'll die up there, boy!" shouted the dead goat.

"Die here, die there," sighed Pike. "I might as well die trying."

Fairmae's voice once again sounded in Pike's head.

They have you well and truly brainwashed, you insolent boy.

"If this is your idea of torment, you've got a lousy imagination," called Pike, mounting the final flight of stairs.

Then I shall just have to relish your death all the more. The words were followed by a shallow laugh; its emptiness made it frightening.

Pike ascended almost casually, even though he knew this might be the last flight of stairs he ever took. At the top he was surprised to see that the landing formed part of a large, open room that covered the entire top floor. The only features of note were the handrails around the square hole of the gallery, and Dan Fairmae.

As predicted by Robyn, Fairmae was standing in a pentacle, which was the least curious thing about him.

He radiated an antiqueness that made even his two-hundred-plus years of life seem like an under estimation. Here was a man who no longer resembled a man. Completely hairless, his skin was flame red, and cracked and crazed all over like parched earth. There was plenty of his skin on display, as he wore nothing but a loin cloth in a fetching gold colour. The cracks were his only discernible facial features. His build was lean, and his skin was drawn taught over is musculature, giving the appearance that one deep breath would cause the cracks to rip open, allowing his innards to spill.

Pike stopped in front of the pentacle, about an arm's length from Fairmae.

So, we meet at last, thought Fairmae.

"Yes, we do," said Pike. "It's not an honour."

Cheeky to the end.

"Yours, not mine, I hope. Do you think you could actually talk to me? I mean, I made the effort to come all this way to see you. What do you say?"

I will do this my way.

"So, what? Your face'll crack if you speak? Is that it?"

Insolent child!

"That is it, isn't it? You can't talk or your face'll fall off. You're a wreck."

He was stopped by a punch in the face. Not that it came physically from Fairmae, but he did cause it. Pike dropped to the ground, dropped his container of moisturiser on the floor and spat blood before wiping his mouth with the back of his hand, leaving it red streaked.

A wreck, eh? Who's the one on the floor, bleeding?

"That'll be me. Now, if you don't mind, I need to remove your heart, but you knew that already." As he finished talking, Pike launched himself at the pentacle—

—and was knocked back down by its protective field.

You can't get to me, Pike. All that effort, all that fighting, and here you are, a useless imbecile.

"Richt ackht slooouk nacht essantenta," he incanted, slowly getting off the floor and readying himself for his next attack.

Pointless even trying. You'll fail and die.

"Better that than to do nothing. Essantenta, essantenta, essantenta."

Once again, he threw himself at the pentacle.

Once again he bounced back to the floor. Things were getting painful.

How much pain can you take?

This was a good point. Launching himself at a pentacle with the assistance of a freeing incantation didn't seem conducive to a pain-free existence. But something occurred to him. Why was Fairmae stuck inside the pentacle at all? If he was so powerful, why wasn't he attacking instead?

"A bit tiring, is it?"

What do you mean, ignorant imp?

"All the magicks you've used so far," replied Pike, getting up and playing for time. "Making the building bigger than it was, controlling the men downstairs – oh, and the child with the rifle-thing, Neat touch that, employing an innocent to threaten me, so that I'd strike him and tarnish my own innocence. But you failed. Then the woman and baby: what on Earth were you thinking, Dan?" All the time, Pike paced around, looking for a weakness but seeing none.

You don't know what you're dealing with. Go back to that pitiful place from whence you came.

"By the gods! You must be really exhausted to suggest you'd let me go. You went to all that trouble to ruin my chances, and it's come down to you being stuck in a bubble and me trying to burst it. I'm surprised: you can keep all these people under control and enslave them, yet you're knackered doing a few cheap tricks to put me off."

Your stupidity is exceeded only by your ugliness.

"Funny," said Pike, circling around Fairmae, still not spotting a way to break the shield, "a few weeks ago that would have upset me, but now it's just empty words. You see, I've learned a few things on my journey here: friendship, courage, tactics, the shallow futility of my existence, all that sort of stuff. I've learned what evil is and what evil isn't: I've even learned how to ride a horse. But out of all the things I've learned, the one thing that makes that kind of insult so laughable is—"

"—DON'T FORGET TO MOISTURISE!" yelled Elf, breathless and panting and at the top of the stairs.

"Yeah, I was going to say that."

"It's a great dictum. You should live by it." Elf nodded towards the container near to Pike's feet.

"And I will, once I've figured out how to restore Moorlock."

"Why wait?" asked Elf. "No time like the present." He nodded a little more forcefully at the moisturiser. "After all, you wouldn't want to go on your victory parade looking like that."

What was it the rifle-boy had said? *Holy oil.*

"You know Elf, you're right. No time like the present."

Pike crouched down, removed the lid, and scraped out the last dregs of ointment. He was about to rub the goo onto his face, but Elf said, "Victory is in your grasp, Pike, and in your blood."

What nonsense do you two speak? demanded Fairmae from within his self-imposed prison.

"Just a few beauty tips. You only get one chance to make a first impression," replied Pike, rubbing the cream onto his hands, mixing it with the blood he had wiped from his mouth. He stood up again. "Right, I'm done." He turned away from the pentacle and took a step towards Elf.

You're leaving? asked Fairmae's voice inside Pike's head.

"Afraid so," said Pike, spinning around and driving his right hand into the magick space, fingers straight out and aimed at Fairmae's heart. "Once I have this!"

Pike's hand passed into the chest cavity with remarkable ease and a loud squelch that was drowned out by Fairmae's scream. He grasped at the only thing that could be a heart and yanked on it, the squeal of his enemy threatening to burst his eardrums. There was resistance as the organ ripped away from the connective tissue.

Just as his hand pulled out of Fairmae's ribcage, Pike felt a searing pain in his gut. He looked down: Fairmae's right arm had transformed into a sword and had impaled him. Pike's blood erupted onto Fairmae, making him scream even louder. Smoke started to rise from the splatters.

Pike fell backwards out of the pentacle, gasping, unable to inhale. Blood filled his lungs, his throat, his mouth. As he stumbled into Elf's arms, Fairmae burst into a pillar of flames.

"The heart," urged Elf, lowering Pike to the floor. "Do you have the heart?"

Weakly, Pike held the still beating organ up for Elf to see.

"Then do your job and say the words!"

Pike gasped, the smell of burning flesh in his nose. How could he speak?

"Say them!"

Pike looked up at Elf's face, which was somehow more familiar now than ever before. Robyn flew onto Elf's shoulder. She was crying.

Birds can't shed tears.

But she cried real tears, and her beautiful face was stained with their tracks. Her beautiful human face. Long blond tresses that cascaded over her shoulders. "Say the words, please?" she whispered.

He blinked, and she was just a sparrow after all.

Say them.

Her voice was soft and warm inside his head. Comforting. She deserved a human face.

"Restorae…"

Elf looked desperate.

"… restorer …" he gasped again, convinced this was his last breath.

"One more, Pike," said Elf, his face contorting strangely. "Just one more."

Pike registered the change and felt that death must surely be upon him.

"… rest … resto … restorus." He finished.

"Thank you," said Elf.

Except, in that last second before death, Pike saw that it was Moorlock.

24: BEFORE THE STORM

There was a familiar sound, and a familiar feeling; a familiar sensation and something that was not familiar.

An ache.

A really bad ache.

He had ached before, but that was in life. Normally after melon harvest.

Was death supposed to be this painful?

Now: a familiar smell.

It was as if he had been transported back to Ooze: the freshness of the air was a distant memory, but he recognised it for what it was.

And it was that.

He was going to haunt Ooze as punishment for failure.

"Did moy lil'tiddler foight like a brave 'un?" sobbed his gran's voice.

Don't cry Gran. I'm not worth it.

There was no way she could hear him.

"Just like his father. Too much of an adventurer, that one."

Mum! I didn't want to leave here, I promise.

"Oi blame you, Moorlock. He upped and left me all those years ago and then he comes back, putting all this stoopid oideas into moy young Pikey-wikey's head."

Left you, Gran? What do you mean?

"You can't blame me, Vilmad. I didn't foretell his future. The Great Book has been around for years. All I did was conceive his father with you – and that was preordained. You must know that – I didn't make it a secret."

Moorlock! You're my grandfather?

Yes, indeed, Moorlock responded.

Cripes! You can talk to ghosts?

No. I mean, yes I can, but you are not a ghost, even though you tried so hard to be one. Come and join us outside. Mind the ladder on the way down.

Pike sat up, aware for the first time that there was more to him than just an ache, and that there was more to the ache than just a minor discomfort.

This hurts like hell!

Yes, so it should. You died momentarily. I exhausted myself putting you back together – had to chase your soul all around the top floor of City Hall to catch it. The healing process can be a tad painful, but you won't burst open by moving around: my spells hold better than that.

Pike fell down the ladder. He was in Gran's house, and he was alive. He knew he had died, but he really was alive – he could tell by the freshly forming bruise on his arm.

He found the warlock outside, seated on a barrel. Moorlock grinned. "Didn't I say mind the ladder?"

Gran was also on a barrel, while his mother was crouched and leaning against the wall of Gran's house.

"Hello Pike," said his mum. She was wearing a new melon skin bonnet, and she looked a mess, but that was normal for her.

"Hello Mum, Moorlock, Gran. Anyone care to tell me what's going on?" His innards ached like crazy, aggravated by the fall, but the sight of his relatives was a relief.

"Oh, moy little Pike," sobbed Gran, deftly launching herself at him from the barrel. "Oi knew you could be chosen, but Oi never thought it'd 'appen." She flung her arms around him and squeezed tightly.

"Argghh!" said Pike.

"Oh, sorry. Oi forgot," said Gran, releasing him.

Moorlock raised himself from his barrel.

"Vilmad, Bess? Do please excuse us. I think I owe the boy an explanation. Pike, come walk with me. The movement will do you the power of good."

Without question – there was no point in questioning, after what he had been through – Pike walked with the old man. It was a warm day; judging by the position of the sun it was mid-afternoon. They headed towards the fertility stone, because there was no place else to aim for.

"You are feeling rested?" asked Moorlock.

"Sort of. You were Elf, weren't you?"

"Aye, that was me."

"I thought you were imprisoned by your arch enemy."

Moorlock stabbed his staff into the soil in front of him, as if expecting the ground to open up. "I was imprisoned – inside that great oaf's form."

"I liked him, mostly."

"He is kind of lovable, isn't he? And resourceful as well. He was my chosen form when Fairmae tried to kill me. No magicks, but great ability."

"I don't understand."

"There are many things that no one understands, young man, and I'm not sure I do. However, I will tell you what happened.

"I have been employed as the County Warlock for many, many years. A few hundred years ago, well before my time, one of Lord du Well's ancestors took it on himself to be the so-called employer. It seemed harmless enough, so my forebears went along with it." He stopped walking, pressing down on his staff to un-stoop himself. "In fact, it was thought that out of all the families who rose to any importance, the du Well's were the most likely to become corrupt, so being employed by them would provide the ideal early warning mechanism that the International Council of Warlocks, Witches, Wizards and Seers needed."

"The what?" asked Pike, as they continued walking.

"The International Council of Warlocks, Witches, Wizards and Seers. My real bosses."

"You mean there are lots of wizards and you're all organised?"

"That about sums it up, boy. We've always known about the machine age, and that man destroyed most of what was this planet. Much of what you've seen – the Stinking Peat Bogs, the giant sabre-toothed worms – these are not natural phenomena, they are hideous corruptions, brought on by man's stupidity."

"Fusion power?"

"Indeed. Fusion power. We know of this because of what was left behind – their writings, the mess, the deformations of reality. They tore a hole in space and time, you know? That's taken some work to manage, I can tell you. Anyway, the Council have sworn to protect the world from technology and we came up with a plan. Ah, here we are, the Fertility Stone of Ooze."

They entered the stone circle and walked towards the unimpressive centre-piece.

"Yeah, where it all started," reflected Pike.

"Where it all started for you, perhaps, but this has been going on for centuries."

They reached the middle and stopped. Pike didn't know what to do, really. Then he decided that the sensation of being alive after knowing that he died was so surreal that all he could do was listen and learn, so he sat on the grass. Moorlock sat on the stone and stood up again abruptly.

"By the gods, young Pike, did you really sit on that thing for hours? It's so sharp and pointy."

"I used a sack."

"An early sign of your potential, I fancy. Where was I? Oh yes. It's been a long and drawn out plan. First we had to come up with a prophecy that was none too specific. We decided – I say we, but it was my predecessors – we decided that there would have to be a hero who could be called into action at the appropriate time. Trouble was, we didn't know when that would be. So, we wrote the Great Book, and we stored it in the Great Hall of Books. We put in some handy pointers and spells, as you found out.

"We then needed to identify who the hero would be, but we had no real idea of when he would be needed. So, the plan was that we Warlocks would sire a blood line from which we could draw when the time was right."

Pike huffed. "And you sired my father and a couple of others with my granny."

"Ah, Vilmad," sighed Moorlock. "Quite beautiful in her time, you know? Mad as a box of drunken winglekrats now, of course, and she's aged dreadfully ... but I digress. For the hero to be activated, he first had to live to the age of seven years, and secondly had to be at the local stone circle at noon on the longest day. We activated twenty or more over the years, and either they were not needed or they were useless failures. Your advantage was that the longest day was also your birthday, so you were imbued with natural powers in addition to the ones you inherited from me. The hero also needed to be totally innocent and alive at his sixteenth birthday. I have to tell you that as plans go, ours was full of holes, but we compensated by siring lots of descendents."

"How did you speak to me from within the stone?"

"Nothing mysterious there, young man. These circles, or ones like them, predate even the machine age by thousands of years. Ancient man built them on ley lines – natural points of communication that encircle the Earth. The principal of communication requires no magick powers, just knowledge of how they work. I had merged with Elf by the time of your sixteenth birthday, so I had to use the stone. The stones are honest things; they would only ever convey my true being, not that of Elf, so you heard me speaking to you."

The sun had lowered, and the breeze grew cool. Pike's torso still ached, but he was beginning to feel a little more vibrant. He shuffled around. Moorlock looked tired now. Perhaps the effort of being Elf and then transforming back had taken its toll.

"How did you become Elf, and why?"

"Fairmae knew about the Council's plans – he used to be part of it."

"What?"

"He was a warlock like me. He went renegade after he failed to sire a bloodline. That was another weak spot in our plans, but magick is never a precise art when it comes to long term planning and prophecies. He mastered the dark arts and then made them darker. The Council was slow to respond and his powers became far too great for us to handle. Then he started picking us off, one by one. He killed at least three quarters of our number and then tried to kill me. He nearly succeeded, but I had anticipated his move and had an alternative defence – Elf. Fairmae worked by tracking down energy fields. I radiate energy because I'm so damned powerful. When he sent his demons to kill me I merged with Elf: no magical powers, but lots of guile and cunning. Big, too. Once I had escaped into Elf I was trapped in that form.

"You see, having these powers takes its toll: Elf is what I could have been if I hadn't been me. Using powers in the way that we warlocks do just drains the life out of you."

"Does that mean I'm on the slope down to being a wreck?"

"You? Why on earth would you think that? You're not a warlock."

"But I used magicks to defeat Fairmae."

"Power, my friend, some of it was borrowed power. We will lend you some more if it's needed – plus you have my blood, so there's a natural aptitude there. No, only if you dedicate your life to the art does it damage you: that's why it had to be someone fresh to defeat him. You do have power, but I doubt you will ever wish to become a warlock. If one of us had tried he would have seized on our ambition and used it against us. As Robyn said, even I am tainted."

"What happened to Scarlet Deadnight?"

"That slippery mare! I killed her twice, yet still she got away. I must have lost my touch. First I got her when I saved Horse, then I got her on the way to save you. The second time she dematerialised when I pushed my blade into her throat. She seems to have mastered a few tricks of the dark arts."

"Where will she have gone?"

"She could only have transported herself to somewhere local. After that, if she didn't bleed to death, she'd have gone back to Fort du Well."

Pike stroked his chin and thought for a while.

"How did you manage to get Lord du Well's chief handmaiden to give me the holy oils? You couldn't possibly have known that he'd capture me."

"With the noise you three were making in the forest it was actually a very safe bet. A while back, in my current form, I had a liaison with Lily. With her I sired a separate bloodline from yours. Consequently, as Elf, I knew how to find her, and I found her once your capture was confirmed. I told her that Moorlock intended for you to have the moisturiser and she accepted it without question. I know what du Well is like, his ambitions and greed are legendary, and I also knew of his vanity. He has a habit of sharing his beauty tips, but if he hadn't volunteered Lily's services she would have given you the cream in any event."

"The container it was stored in: it had the word Too-per-warie on it. Is that some kind of magick holy word?"

"No, that's Tupperware, and it's the name of the box. It's one of the many things Fairmae supplied to du Well to keep him onside. Du Well is a weakling, but easy to control. Fairmae nurtured a lot of other allies with his gifts; doubtless you'll meet them in due course."

"Where is Robyn – and Horse? Are they OK?"

"All in good time. Albanroot, however, stayed at the Pit of Zidor. He decided to use his caring nature to help those people."

They sat in silence for a while. Pike pondered what he had been told, and what he hadn't.

"Tell me, grandfather, if it was you who left the Great Book at the toll booth, why did Elf – you – try to stop me from reading it?"

"Elf had to delay your powers. If you had attained them too soon then Fairmae would have sensed you and stopped you. If you had read out the memory spell and absorbed everything, say, in the Peat Bogs, you'd never have reached the other side."

"Can the memory spell be reversed? Right now I can remember every breath I've ever taken. I remember grazing my knee as a child and the pain it caused. I think most of the ache I feel inside is because of that spell."

"Yes, I'll reverse it."

Moorlock brushed his fingertips across Pike's forehead.

"How does that feel?"

Pike breathed in deeply and tried to think of his birth. Strangely, he could remember remembering it, but he couldn't remember the event itself. He smiled.

"I think that worked. So what did Fairmae want? Why was he excavating the city?"

"He was ambitious, most of we warlocks are. But most of us plough our ambitions into defeating evil while he ploughed his into propagating it. I told you that man tore a hole in space and time, didn't I? Well it's a tiny thing that requires a patch every now and then. It takes a lot of effort to plug it up. He wanted to expand it, and to become the lord of chaos. He wanted to own everything, to control evil. There's no sense to it, no logic, just greed and ambition."

"And I – we – stopped him, so the world is safe."

"For now. But there are others who are not yet as powerful as Fairmae who wish to resurrect the machines and to take power and rule the world. If they succeed then they will complete Fairmae's work. We must be ready to fight them when the time arises."

"When will that be?"

"It could be soon, or maybe not in your lifetime. Who knows? Lord du Well may appear to be a harmless idiot, but he's well connected and was part of Fairmae's strategy to rule the world. He's not going to give up easily. I think we are in the calm before the storm."

They returned to the village in silence. Pike tried to rationalise all that had happened, and all that he had been told. It seemed incredible now that he had wandered the world and saved it. Back here he felt he was just a melon farmer. One with a headache.

There was a bit of a commotion going on when they reached the dirt track that was the main – and only – street. Makeshift tables had been erected along the building lines and chairs were placed all around. Gran was scuttling back and forth, barking crazed commands at the villagers. A sacred beast trotted backwards and forwards along the line of tables, pinching bits of food from them; no one except Gran paid it any heed.

"Gerrof thur, ya filthy thieving mule! Thought we'd seen the last of ya when Pike rode off into the night."

"Horse?" called Pike.

The beast stopped nibbling and trotted over to greet him.

"Ah, Pike. I see you are alive. Nice."

Pike threw his arms around Horse's neck.

"A-hem. You said you wouldn't squeeze that hard if we met again."

"I lied!" sobbed Pike, tears of joy spilling down his cheeks.

"Your eyes are leaking."

"I know. Where's Robyn."

I'm here.

The sparrow landed on Pike's left shoulder and pecked his ear lobe painfully.

"Ouch!"

"That's for dying! Don't do it again."

"I'll try not to."

Moorlock slapped his shoulder. "And I'll try not to let you."

"One thing you didn't tell me, grandfather: how did we get back here?"

"Warlock travel. No great shakes."

The villagers began to assemble around the tables, all looking at Pike. He stroked his chin, wondering if it was flaky again. But it wasn't.

"They all know what you've done," said Robyn. "Your gran has the loudest mouth ever."

"When I was about to die, I saw you."

"Well, I was there with you, so you would."

"I mean, I saw the real you."

"You think? We'll see."

Gran somehow managed to climb onto a table that seemed barely able to carry her weight. She clanged a spoon against a dish until everyone was silent.

"Roight ev'rywun! My grandson, lil' ol' Pike, has saved the world from chaos, so we're 'avin' a celebration. LET'S PAAR-TEEEEE!

And they did.

~ THE END? ~

COMING LATE 2012

Pike's ReQuest

Join Pike in his continuing quest.

Read on for a sample chapter ...

A FRIEND BECOMES FOE

Autumn – 911 ND - The Badlands of Abergravan: in a bar, just before dawn

The bartender looked at the crumpled stranger with disdain. Here was a man who had seen the wrong side of life, and make no mistake. Shame he insisted on resting his flea-ridden beard on the counter, but a paying customer was a paying customer no matter how much wildlife he carried around with him.

"So, what can I get for you, my verminous friend?"

The stranger – who had crawled, rather than walked, in – scratched his hairy chin and replied, "I'm no one's friend." His voice was gruff and bitter sounding.

"Suit yourself, but I can hardly go around saying, 'so what can I get for you, my verminous', can I? That'd just be plain rude, that would."

The stranger belched loudly, but otherwise made no reply. There was no echo; the room was made of twigs, dried grasses and mud, put about a wooden frame that looked no more sturdy than the legs of a crane fly.

"Come on, big chap, what do you want?" He sniffed. "This is a bar, you know? I can't just have malingerers chocking up the place, resting their faces on the counter and stinking so badly that all the other customers run away."

The man raised his head slowly, looking around the almost empty room, as if wondering where these departing customers could be. The only other beings in the room were a dog with more fleas than the stranger, and the bartender.

"Counter?"

"Counter."

The bartender was proud of his counter: he had made it from scraps of wood he had collected in the foot hills of the Abergravan mountains, and had spent many hours smoothing and polishing the planks after joining them to a rough frame made of anything he could get hold of. The result was an unsightly mess, but it was his unsightly mess and no one could say otherwise.

"Come on then, oh verminous stinker who is friend to no one: what do you want?"

The man's head slowly began to rise up. At first the barman thought it was some ungodly act of levitation, but soon he realised that the stranger was beginning to stand.

"What do I want?" mumbled the man, as if to himself. "I want my life back, that's what I want. I want to know who stole the last few weeks; who made me do those strange things and feel those strange feelings. I want to know who Pike is, and why I trusted him and called him master …" He now stood at his full height, or he would have done if the roof had been high enough to permit it. He continued, his voice rising gradually. "I want to find this Pike, and someone called Moorlock. I want to find those who assisted them to make my life a misery–" his voice grew to a roar "–and then I want to KILL – THEM – ALL!" He slammed his fist onto the countertop with his last word: the entire construction collapsed with a loud crash, causing the dog to yelp and run out through the reed matting that constituted a door.

The barman, trembling, said, "And, erm, to drink?"

The Village of Ooze – same time

Pike didn't know what a hangover was until the day he woke up with one. Someone had told him that consuming large quantities of ale along with chasers of fermented watermelon juice was good for his constitution. The conversation went like this:

> ***PERSON WHOSE NAME PIKE COULDN'T REMEMBER (PWNPCR):*** Drink long and plentifully, young Pike, for you have come of age some two years sooner than most.
>
> ***PIKE:*** But I'm too young for hard liquor. It's against village rules at my age.
>
> ***PWNPCR:*** Old enough to save the world and defeat cunning evil, old enough to quaff masses of fermented melon juice and ale, is what I say, and I sit on the village council and help make the village rules. It'll do a young fellow like you the power of good.

To some extent, Pike agreed. In the weeks before the party he had transformed from timid melon farmer to saviour of all that was right. He had travelled across the country on horseback – unheard of in modern times – in company with a talking sparrow named Robyn, a shepherd called Albanroot, and a huge warrior named Elf who turned out to be Moorlock the Warlock in disguise. Together they had faced the greatest hardships, including fights with giant sabre-toothed worms, one-eye winglekrats, bog creatures, man-eating flowers and, not least, the most evil being in creation – Dan Fairmae – whose heart Pike had ripped from his chest in order to release Moorlock from his incarceration in the body of Elf. Of course, had Pike known beforehand that winning the heart of a fair maiden meant tearing the heart out of Dan Fairmae he might never have started out on his quest, but ultimately he had knowingly faced evil and had won. Surely, a little drink to celebrate wouldn't do him any harm?

Except, of course, when he was staying as guest of honour in his Gran's house.

Gran was in the habit of waking just before dawn. It didn't matter what time of year it was, if dawn arrived she would be there to greet it. This meant that in the winter months she was barely awake at all, and in summer she hardly slept. And if Gran was awake in her own home, anyone else there would be as well. Normally, Pike wouldn't have minded too much, but Gran was prodding him with a stick.

"PIKE, yer lazy kipper! Wake up and keep yer ol' gran company. It's nearly daylight," she called from downstairs, jabbing at him.

It was a long stick that she used; it passed up between the floorboards of the wooden platform that was the upstairs floor. Pike could feel it prodding away between his shoulder blades, the straw mattress on which he lay giving him practically no protection.

"It was nearly daylight when I got to bed. Leave me be," he groaned.

"Leave 'ee be? Leave 'ee be? Just 'cos 'ee stopped evil from sweeping cross the known world, moy li'l tiddler thinks 'ee can abandon his ol' Gran, 'ee duz. Oh!" she sobbed, "What will become of me?"

Pike grunted – half a snore, really – and realised he was defeated when the stick tore through the sack cloth encasing the straw, and scraped the bare flesh of his back. He was momentarily reminded of Lord du Well prodding him when he was forced to act as lead shepherd at the front of the Lord's sheep-drawn buggy.

"By the power of Adriarch, Gran," he snapped, "stop poking me. I've had enough of that for a lifetime."

"Well get 'ee's rump down 'ere and I won't 'ave to do it," she snapped, giving one more sharp prod.

Pike yelped and sat up rapidly. And that was when he knew what a hangover was: bad, really, really bad.

The throbbing of blood pumping through the constricted blood vessels of his brain was more painful than anything he had experienced on his adventure, and the sweating was almost as bad as anything he had experienced while fighting strange creatures and wearing full body armour. And the thirst … how could he possibly be dehydrated after the amount of ale he had imbibed up to an hour before now?

Pike stood, smashing his head against a cross-member of the roof – "Argghh!" – and staggered towards the rickety ladder down which he fell to the ground floor. His landing wasn't too bad so he closed his eyes and stayed there. He was reawakened by a bucket of cold water.

"Wha –?"

"Dawn, moy li'l tiddler. Come and watch the sunrise. It's able to rise because of you. Come see it."

And in that moment, half-drunk, fully hung-over, drenched and dehydrated, he realised just what he had achieved.

The Badlands of Abergravan: in a bar – sunrise

"ALE! GIVE ME ALE? What else would I want?"

The bartender grabbed a leather tankard and filled it from a barrel that was mounted on a stand behind what used to be the counter.

"Ale. Of course. What else? Here you are, oh huge man with attitude. I trust you will be paying for the ale and the damage?"

The stranger grabbed the tankard and emptied it in one gulp.

"More!"

"Payment?" asked the bartender, shaking, as he took back the drinking vessel.

"You'll get your due. More ale."

Feeling calmer, the bartender refilled the tankard. Passing it back, he said, "Let's sit. The day is young and I have no other customers. I don't sleep until after sunrise, so you can tell me all your troubles." He sat down on a log on the public side of the bar and indicated to a larger one nearby. The massive, hairy stranger sat and sighed. He drank again, but this time without desperation.

"Speak, my huge and sweaty non-friend. I believe you mentioned strange actions and strange feelings?"

With gleaming eyes, the stranger looked over the rim of the tankard at the bartender.

"Aye, indeed. Feelings unbefitting a man of my status: feelings of loyalty and friendship. Actions for which I was not ever going to be paid and for which I had no desire to be paid."

"What on earth is your status, that loyalty and friendship are considered unbefitting? These are surely fine attributes for any man?"

"Any man but a soldier of fortune. MORE ALE!"

The barman got more ale, and hoped that his payment would shortly follow. He sat again.

"Surely, even a mercenary may show loyalty? Why would anyone employ you if you were incapable of it?"

"A fair but flawed point," grunted the stranger. "Loyalty is awarded to the highest bidder – or if not the highest, the one who makes the offer of payment first. We mercenaries have a code of ethics, and working loyally for free is not in it."

"Perhaps you are the innovator of a new code?"

"Never! The code is the code. I am no innovator; I am a criminal in the eyes of other soldiers of fortune – or I would be, if ever they find out about me before I avenge myself."

The barman began to sense something. His stomach knotted as the merest hint of what was to become crossed his mind. Showing no outward sign of unease, he asked: "More ale, sir? Last one's on the house."

"Aye, more ale."

The tankard was passed from one to the other, filled, and passed back.

"Thank you," said the stranger. "It is good that you show me this small kindness. You may wish to know my name."

Now the barman knew there was a problem.

"No, oh strange, muscly and gigantic one with the very sharp-looking weaponry. I think that is not a good idea."

"Why ever not? You have asked after my affairs and I have confided in you. It's fair you should know who I am."

"No. Most kind of you, but I am a barman and I always pry into the affairs of strangers. It is the way of my kind … part of our code, if you will. I wouldn't wish to know your name, as I wouldn't wish to blab it unintentionally."

The stranger rose up from his seat having drained his tankard. He cast the leather vessel to one side and stood till his head touched the straw roofing.

"There is only one like me, so I may as well introduce myself—"

"La-la-la-la-la-not-listening!" squealed the bartender, leaping up and stuffing his fingers into his ears.

"You will listen," shouted the large man, leaning forward and pulling the bartender's fingers away from his ears. "My name is—"

"No! Tell me not. Your secrets are safe with me. Don't tell me. La-la-la-la—"

"ELF!"

The bartender exhaled loudly. "You shouldn't have told me."

"I should. And now to give you your due."

The dagger glinted momentarily in the lamp-light before piercing the bartender's heart.

+++

AFTERWORD

Hello, nice to meet you.

There are reasons for this book being self published, and here are some of them.

I tried to get this book brought to the attention of a publisher or two, but most publishers will not accept submissions directly from authors – I needed an agent.

Many UK agents don't accept any submissions that involve fantasy, sci-fi, an element of young adult content or anything involving animals that speak. Out of all the twenty or so agents who did read *Pike's Quest*, not one of them had a bad word for it. Many of them actually lavished praise upon it – they just didn't want any new clients, or they couldn't see a market for it in an already over-crowded marketplace. One agent told me that although I write beautifully, and that *Pike's Quest* was the best-written submission she had seen all year, she couldn't take me on as a client.

I did manage to get two publishers to read Pike: Barry Cunningham, of *The Chicken House*, read it before I submitted it to any agents. He really enjoyed it, but thought the wordplay and humour was too complex for his readership. He urged me to submit elsewhere. This was high praise, what with Barry being the man who signed JK Rowling to Bloomsbury. One other publisher also read it and enjoyed parts of it, but didn't like the way I had written -

(a) Gran's west-country accent and

(b) du Well's speech impediment.

In the case of **(a)**, tough! I decided on her speech patterns after seeing the *Lord of the Rings* movies, and being amused that Samwise Gamgee came from the same small village as Frodo and company, yet was the only Hobbit with a strong Somerset accent. I somehow found it more amusing than the Scottish and Manchester accents used by Merry and Pippin!

In the case of **(b)**, again I say tough. I wanted him to be a laughable buffoon, but a dangerous one. Much of the humour is based around his speech patterns, and he didn't play a massively intrusive role (and I offer my apologies to anyone who has a lisp – no offence is intended).

If you have enjoyed reading *Pike's Quest* you let me know. E-mail me at writer@kjbennett.co.uk

I thank you for reading Pike's Quest, and for your indulgence.

Kevin ~ June 2012

=

Websites
http://www.kjbennett.co.uk
http://kj-bennett.blogspot.com
http://pikequest.blogspot.com

E-mail
pike@kjbennett.co.uk

Follow me on Twitter
@kj_bennett

Find/Like
Pike's Quest
on Facebook
http://www.facebook.com/pages/Pikes-Quest/217399291625570

Printed in Great Britain
by Amazon.co.uk, Ltd.,
Marston Gate.